Nic[illegible] a woman could possibly wish for in a man.

If a man, and marriage, were what the woman wanted.

But it wasn't. Not for Beth. She couldn't afford to relinquish even a small part of herself to a man ever again. Not now. Not ever.

Reaching up, Beth touched Nick's cheek. Nick thought he saw regret in her eyes, but maybe that was just wishful thinking because she said, "Thank you," softly, but with unmistakable implacability.

"You're a good man, but marriage is out of the question."

"It doesn't have to be." Nick didn't budge. Her palm against his cheek warmed him. He mourned the loss of that warmth when she took the hand away. "It could work for us. I'm not like him, Elizabeth."

"I know that. But I don't love you, Nick. And given my history, I doubt I ever could."

Dear Reader,

This month, wedding bells ring for six couples who marry for convenient reasons—and discover love by surprise. Join us for their HASTY WEDDINGS.

Kasey Michaels starts off the month with *Timely Matrimony,* a love story with a time-travel twist. It's all in the timing for modern-day bride Suzi Harper, and Harry Wilde, her handsome husband from the nineteenth century. Just as they found happiness, it seemed Harry's destiny was to leave her....

In Anne Peters's *McCullough's Bride,* handsome rancher Nick McCullough rescues single mom Beth Coleman the only way he knows how—he marries her! Now Nick is the one in danger—of losing his heart to a woman who could never return his love.

Popular Desire author Cathie Linz weaves a *One of a Kind Marriage.* In this fast-paced romp, Jenny Benjamin and Rafe Murphy start as enemies, then become man and wife. Marriage may have solved their problems, but can love cure their differences?

The impromptu nuptials continue with *Oh, Baby!,* Lauryn Chandler's humorous look at a single woman who is determined to have a child—and lands herself a husband in the bargain. It's a green card marriage for Kelsey Shepherd and Frankie Falco in *Temporary Groom.* Jayne Addison continues her Falco Family series with this story of short-term commitment—and unending attraction! The laughter continues with Carolyn Zane's *Wife in Name Only*—a tale of marriage—under false pretenses.

I hope you enjoy our HASTY WEDDINGS. In the coming months, look for more books by your favorite authors.

Happy reading,

Anne Canadeo
Senior Editor

McCULLOUGH'S BRIDE

Anne Peters

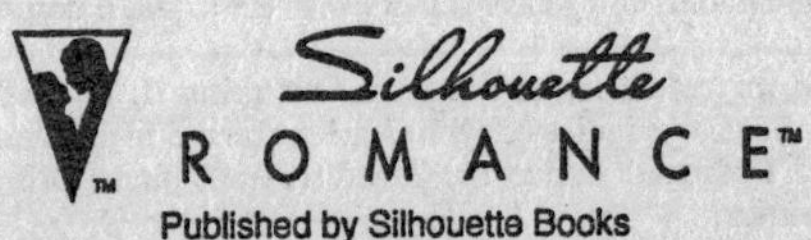

Published by Silhouette Books
America's Publisher of Contemporary Romance

This one is for you, Mary Theresa.
Without your ongoing help and encouragement,
most of my stories would never see the
printed page.

ISBN 0-373-19031-X

McCULLOUGH'S BRIDE

This edition published by arrangement with Harlequin Enterprises B. V.

Printed in U.S.A.

Books by Anne Peters

Silhouette Romance

Through Thick and Thin #739
Next Stop: Marriage #803
And Daddy Makes Three #821
Storky Jones Is Back in Town #850
Nobody's Perfect #875
The Real Malloy #899
The Pursuit of Happiness #927
Accidental Dad #946
His Only Deception #995
McCullough's Bride #1031

Silhouette Desire

Like Wildfire #497

ANNE PETERS

makes her home in the Pacific Northwest with her husband and their dog, Adrienne. Family and friends, reading, writing and travel—those are the things she loves most. Not always in that order, not always with equal fervor, but always without exception.

Beth Coleman's Thoughts On Marriage:

Marry in haste and in leisure repent.
Isn't that how the saying goes?
Just between me and you
This doesn't have to be true.
It depends on the bridegroom you chose.

If he's good and he's strong
When for security you long,
Then you've chosen wisely and well.
But if he's weak, worn and wimpy,
If means and character are skimpy,
Your marriage could indeed become a prison cell.

So watch whom you choose,
And consider what you'll lose
If an error in judgment you make.
For to in leisure repent because you married in haste
Would be a waste of your life. 'Twould be a waste.

Chapter One

The first thing Dominick McCullough noticed about Nedda's new waitress, was her eyes. Not their color. They were hazel, like a lot of other eyes. Nor was it their size, shape or the length of her lashes that struck him, though all of those things were just fine. No, what Nick noticed, was that they had died.

There was no life in them.

Not that they were blank in a way that bespoke a lack of intelligence; it wasn't like that. It was more like shades had been pulled down over them the way window shades were drawn in houses to keep out the light.

Or keep it in.

She was giving him a professional smile, order pad and pencil at the ready, but those invisible shades kept the smile from being reflected in her eyes. "What'll you have, sir?"

Sir? Faintly amused by this—for Starville, Washington—unorthodox form of address, Nick's lips twitched.

"Today's breakfast special is a Western omelette with home fries and—"

"Just coffee'll do."

"Oh. All right." The pad lowered. Once again their gazes met. Which was when Nick realized, with a peculiar little jolt, that her eyes weren't dead at all. They were sad. They were filled with a sadness so dark and vast that there wasn't room in them for anything else.

That sadness touched him like nothing in the past five years had been able to, or maybe even before that. For sure it nudged something in the vicinity of his heart and told him here was a creature who'd known the kind of pain he himself had known.

Only hers was newer, fresher. The pain in her eyes spoke of wounds that hadn't even crusted over yet, while his own only rarely festered anymore.

Nick heaved a sigh, cursing life and its cruel ways, but reminding himself that bellyaching about it wouldn't change a damn thing. And that the last thing he had time for was to worry about somebody else's grief. He'd have grief of his own waiting for him at the bank in Spokane if he failed to convince its president of how crucial that additional range land—and the creek that traversed it—would be to the Triple Creek Ranch. He'd been after old man Sawyer to sell it to him for years, but the sodden old coot had been too cantankerous to play ball. Well, now he was dead and buried, without widow or heirs, and the government was selling his land for back taxes.

Which only went to show that a man's whole life didn't amount to a hill o' beans if he didn't have kin or an heir.

Nick had no heir, either, but he did have family. Plenty of family, and all pretty well within hailing distance from the Triple Creek.

The two-thousand-acre spread had been the McCullough family seat for more than four generations. The first Dominick McCullough had come west with his new bride, Sarah, right after the turn of the century.

Only two creeks ran through the property, but Dominick McCullough I, being an optimistic sort, had felt sure he'd be able to acquire the land that had creek number three on it just as soon as he had the money. He had cockily called his ranch the Triple Creek in anticipation of the purchase. And each succeeding McCullough had futilely tried to buy the land ever since.

With the bank's help, Dominick McCullough IV finally would. *If* he got a move on and made the ten o'clock appointment that was some two hours' drive away!

"Make that to go," Nick called after the waitress, sliding out of the booth with a grimace of pain. Damn hip. He tossed a dollar on the table for a tip. Too much, but what the hell. The woman'd have to be pretty hard-up to come to this town for a job.

"Mornin', Nick," said Nedda, at the cash register. She was the owner of Nedda's Diner and, at forty-five, going gray around the edges, just as Nick was. Aeons ago they'd gone to school together and had even groped each other in the back seat of Buster Mason's old Chevy once or twice.

"What're you doin' in town so early?" She took the dollar bill he offered and handed back change.

Nick tossed the coins into the can marked Feed The Hungry that sat next to the register and stuck a toothpick between his teeth. "Got to get to Spokane for a coupla days."

"Well, that explains the fancy duds, then." Nedda cast an appreciative look at his gray, Western-cut suit and dress Stetson. "Bi'ness or pleasure?"

He let the wry look he shot her speak for itself.

Nedda laughed, unperturbed by the silent invitation to mind her own business. "You know what they say about all work and no play, Nick...."

"Leave it, Nedda."

"Yeah." It came out as a sigh. "Well, here comes your coffee."

With a brisk, "Thanks, Elizabeth," she relieved the sad-eyed waitress of the foam container and handed it to Nick.

Elizabeth. Nick glanced at the waitress and decided the name suited her. Kind of soft and classy, just like the woman herse—

Damn foolishness. Mad at himself for his lapse into fanciful musings about a woman he neither knew nor had any reason for wanting to know, Nick touched the brim of his hat and, with a curt, "Ladies," limped out of the diner.

Watching him, Nedda sadly shook her head. "Damn shame, a man like that goin' to waste."

She glanced at Beth, who was also staring after the tall, broad-shouldered rancher whose piercing blue gaze had earlier drilled into her in a most disconcerting way.

"Who is he?" Beth asked, surprising herself. What difference did it make? She wasn't about to make friends, or even acquaintances in this town if she could help it. It would be neither smart nor safe.

Nedda's gaze took on a knowing glint. "A lot o' man, ain't he?"

Beth flushed, chagrined that Nedda had apparently misconstrued her idle question. "Oh, I didn't mean—"

"Don't worry, dearie." Nedda patted Beth's arm, a rich chuckle making her ample bosom shake like underdone jelly. "Wouldn't matter if you did. Dominick Bronson McCullough's not up for grabs, more's the pity."

Up for grabs. Beth inwardly winced. Nedda was making the poor man sound like a piece of sale merchandise. She started to protest again. "Well, I certainly didn't—"

But Nedda cut her short. "Then you're one of a kind, hon."

Business became too brisk for chitchat after that. Nedda's was the only eatery in Starville and as such the social hub. As ranchers, wives and hands came into town on errands and such, they invariably stopped in at the diner for a bite and a jaw with neighbors and friends.

It was after one, and Beth had been on her feet since seven that morning, when at last there was enough of a lull to allow her time for her own lunch. There was an ache in the small of her back, her feet throbbed and so did her head as she put her plate with the meat loaf special and a cup of hot tea on the table of the rearmost booth.

"Mind if I join you?" she asked Charley Rider, the cook, who was already sitting there eating.

His mouth full, he waved his fork in silent invitation and Beth gratefully slid into the booth. Too tired to dig into her own food right away, she wearily propped her elbows on the table and put her face in her hands. Her tremulous sigh, as her fingers massaged her forehead, wrung a hacking chuckle-cum-cough out of the cook whose bald pate and ballooning midsection made him resemble a kindly Buddha.

"Pretty new t'all this, ain'tcha?" he asked, thoughtfully chewing and watching her. "Waitin' tables, I mean."

Beth dropped her hands, her "Hmm" response noncommittal. Or so she hoped. She had told Nedda she'd had experience. And she really needed this job. She picked up her fork and stabbed at the food. "It's been a busy morning."

"No more so today'n other days, you'll come to find out." Charley washed his last bite down with a swallow of coffee. "So how's the room at Myrna's suit ya?"

"Just fine." Beth forced another bite of meat loaf down her rebellious throat. She was too wrung-out to be hungry, too weary to eat; only the knowledge that she needed food to keep up her strength, and that she'd need all the strength she could get for the struggles yet to come, made her even make the effort.

"Told ya it weren't much." The note of defensiveness in Charley's voice was obviously a reaction to Beth's sparse reply and general lack of animation. "But it's clean, ain't it? And cheap..."

"It's great. Really." Beth dragged a smile and a note of enthusiasm up from somewhere. "So's your meat loaf, by the way."

The compliment instantly restored Charley's good humor. "Liked it m'self, thank you, ma'am," he said. Then he added, "Though Nedda's pies ain't half bad, neither," around a mouthful of lemon meringue.

He thoughtfully studied Beth again as he chased the bite of pie with another swallow of coffee. "Coleman..." His brows beetled. "Used to know some Colemans in Butte, Montana. Kin o' yours, by any chance?"

"No." Beth kept her eyes on her plate, sliced off another bite of meat loaf and turned the question back to him, all without turning crimson with nerves. She congratulated herself on that since prevarication had never been her forte. "Is Butte your hometown, Mr. Rider?"

"Nope." It seemed the cook, too, had secrets to keep, if his lack of elaboration was any indication. "An' we ain't so formal around here. Plain Charley'll do."

In another life, Beth wouldn't have missed this chance to tease. She would have come back with a laughing, "As you wish, Plain Charley."

But in this life she barely managed a smile to go along with her polite little, "Thank you. And I'm Beth."

Her shift ended at three. Ducking her chin into her coat collar against the bite of the early-December wind, Beth quickly walked the few blocks to the rambling, gone-to-seed Victorian in which—on Charley Rider's recommendation—she had rented an attic room the previous day.

Grateful not to encounter the talkative Myrna, her landlady, or one of the other three tenants in the spacious, wood-paneled entry, Beth climbed the two flights of stairs to her dormer room as fast as her weary legs allowed.

She was exhausted clear down to the marrow, but filled with a grim kind of satisfaction, too. She had done it. She had lasted a whole day at a job. She'd broken only one glass, and she'd only mixed up orders twice. Not bad for a woman whose only food-service experience, aside from serving meals to her family and occasional guests, had been a high school job at McDonald's some eighteen years ago.

The room was as she remembered it—nothing much, but homey in a drab sort of way. A bed, a nightstand, a dresser with a frameless dime-store mirror above it. A table and two chairs in the housekeeping corner that sported a two-burner hot plate below two shelves of serviceable crockery, and above some shelves of blackened pots and pans.

By the time she'd hauled her suitcases up the two flights of stairs the day before it had been dark. She'd had been too tired to pay much attention to anything beyond the fact that the bed had a new mattress and that her sheets fit. Other than that she'd only taken time to dig out the patchwork quilt Granny Coleman had fashioned years ago for Beth's hope chest—and, boy, how Beth had hoped in those days that J. C. Christofferson would soon pop the question.

Banishing thoughts of J.C., she had spread the quilt on the bed and, emotionally and physically running on empty, had crawled beneath it for some much-needed rest. She had slept like the dead, a major miracle given the fact that sleep had been eluding her ever since her goodbyes from Jason.

Her inner alarm had roused her at six and so her first full day in Starville, Washington, had begun.

Now it was barely ten hours later and Beth was once again dead on her feet. Her hands shook with fatigue as she carefully hung up her cashmere coat. It was a good thing Myrna, Nedda and the few others she'd met here in Starville didn't have an eye for such things, or they'd know that all of her understated wardrobe bore very pricey labels. And they'd wonder.

The trappings of the good life, people who did recognize designer styles and quality would say. Knowing better, Beth absently smoothed the sleeve of her coat, her inward smile no more than a bitter parody.

She closed her eyes against the rush of painful memories that assailed her whenever weariness became stronger than her iron resolve to bury the past, to only look forward. Waves of longing suffused her. Her knees quaked. She fiercely pressed her fingers against her eyelids, but too late. Tears erupted from her soul with all the heat and force of a geyser shooting up from the bowels of the earth.

"Oh, Jason..."

With a choked sob, Beth sank to the floor and let grief momentarily claim her....

"Where're we going, Mom?"

Beth and Jason were on the bus, on the interstate, and headed east. Away from Chicago. Away from home.

"We're going to see Kathy, sweetheart."

"Aw, Mom... Why do we have to?"

"Hush now, Jason. We've been over this so many times...."

"Yeah, but why can't I stay with *you,* Mom? Who's gonna take care of *you?* You said I was the man of the house after Dad— After the last time he—"

"Shh, sweetie, shh. Remember we weren't going to talk about that anymore.... Momma loves you, sweetheart."

"Is Kathy gonna read me stories, Mom?"

"You're old enough to read your own stories now, Jason."

"Yeah, but I like listening to 'em better."

"Lazybones."

"I love you, Momma. How long do I gotta stay at Kathy's?"

"Not long, sweetheart. Not long. Just until Mom can find a place where we can settle down and really have fun."

"Anyplace you are is fun, Mom...."

* * *

Oh, Jason. I miss you so much.

Sick at heart, Beth tipped back her head and stared into the gloominess near the ceiling. Painfully, she swallowed the tears pooling at the back of her throat. Impatient with herself, she wiped the moisture off her face with the heels of her hands. She was going to have to stop this if she was to survive. She would lock Jason into a separate compartment way in the back of her heart and mind and keep him there for as long as it took for her to get their lives on course.

On a new course. A better course. One with a future in which she and her son would never have to be afraid, or separated, again.

Beth wasn't quite as tired at the end of her second day at Nedda's Diner. After getting home, she even got her stuff unpacked. She added touches of her own to make the room homier. The musical jewelry box that had been Grampa Coleman's gift on her sixteenth birthday. When you lifted the lid, it played "The Minute Waltz." Beth could never hear the piece without thinking of him, and that was good. There were only a few pieces of simple jewelry inside it, none of them the fancy trinkets that had invariably been J.C.'s peace offerings.

Once again Beth banished thoughts of J.C., concentrating instead on finding suitable spots for her family pictures. Jason, gap-toothed and grinning. He'd been in first grade in that one. Photos of her parents, dead since she was four which had left Granny and Grampa Coleman to raise Beth and her sister, Vera, whom everyone always called Sissy.

Sissy. How happy she and Marcus looked with baby Lucinda between them. With affectionate care, Beth hung the photo of the Patrucci family on the wall above her nightstand.

They lived in Melbourne, Australia, and if they'd known of Beth's plight, Marcus Patrucci would have sent her money and insisted she come to them. But pride, and a fierce need to stand on her own two feet, after years of never having had autonomy, had kept Beth from asking them for help. She had to do this on her own, in her own way. No matter the price in pain and loneliness. No matter that she couldn't be near her child, the one person in this world she loved above all others.

On Thursday, Beth's third day on the job, Nick McCullough came into the diner again. It was the tail end of the lunch hour, but the place was still humming like a beehive in full production, and Beth had her hands and mind full.

Waiting for Charley to look up so she could place her order, longing for a break, her gaze swept the crowded counter of which she was in charge to see what her chances were of getting a rest anytime soon. She sighed as yet another hungry cowpoke lowered himself onto the vacant stool she'd hoped had been an indication that the end of the rush—and the start of her break—was near. He shoved back his hat and unbuttoned his sheepskin jacket. The coat's darkly weathered condition pretty well matched the skin of the man's face.

He glanced her way, and for just a second their eyes connected. His were very blue and didn't smile, but then, neither did his lips. On the contrary, they tightened forbiddingly as he gave her a little nod of greeting and picked up a menu in obvious dismissal.

That was when Beth realized with a queer little jolt that this wasn't just another cowboy. This was that rancher. The one Nedda said wasn't up for grabs.

Stacy Kusick, one of the other waitresses, elbowed in next to Beth. "Clubhouse on whole wheat with fries, Charley. And a steak san on sourdough, rare."

"Gotcha, Stace," the cook replied. "Hey, whatcha need, Beth?"

"Um..." Incredibly, it took Beth a moment to gather her wits and snap her attention back to Charley. Her face flaming, she tore the order slip off her pad and hurriedly clipped it with a forced little laugh. "I—I'm sorry, Charley. My mind went blank there for a second."

"Time for a break, I reckon."

"Must be. I need a Swiss steak special, medium with mashed, hold the broccoli. Chef salad, and a deluxe burger with extra onions 'n' fries."

"Doin' good, kid."

"Thank you." Charley's grudging praise warmed Beth out of all proportion. The big smile she gave him as she took an earlier order in hand visibly dazzled the cook who clapped a hand to his heart in a comic imitation of the stricken swain, making her laugh aloud.

Hearing a musical trill of laughter, Nick glanced up from the menu he hadn't really been studying and caught the tail end of Beth's smile. The sweetness of it hit him like a punch in the solar plexus, making his stomach muscles clench.

For the past two days he'd been telling himself this woman was just that—a woman. One who'd blown into town from who knew where and would, no doubt, shortly be blowing back out of it again. A woman who, if he were smart, he wouldn't lose any sleep over.

And yet he had.

Chapter Two

Nick tore his eyes away from Beth and frowned into the menu again, not any happier with himself now than he had been the day before. Or the one before that. Hell, he'd gotten the damn loan, no sweat, and by rights he should've stayed in Spokane. He should've dropped in on Helen and done a bit of celebrating. But, no, he couldn't wait to hightail it back to Starville. Back to this woman he knew nothing about except her name. Her first name. Elizabeth.

That name had been humming in his head for two days like one of those tunes you couldn't shake no matter what else was going on. And that was bothering him. Bothering him plenty. But not so much that it made him stay away, even though he knew deep in his bones that here was a woman who could hurt him.

Not that he couldn't handle pain as well as any man could. He'd handled his share and then some. But that didn't mean he should welcome it, or be fool enough to go looking for it.

Not that he'd done either where this Elizabeth was concerned. The woman had showed up unbidden, the way most things—trouble and otherwise—had a habit of doing. He hadn't invited her and he hadn't gone looking for her. All he had done and was doing, or so he told himself, was not avoid her and whatever her appearance might come to mean.

Nick grimly snapped the menu and once again forced himself to concentrate on the food-stained words there, all the while thinking, Why're you sticking your neck out, McCullough?

"Beth, take your break," Nedda barked from her post by the cash register.

"I was just going to..." Beth gestured toward Nick, at a loss for his name.

"Stace'll get him." Nedda's tone brooked no further discussion. She said, "Howdy, Nick," and turned back to Beth. "You'll screw up the schedule if you don't take your break now, so git."

Beth shrugged. Fine. Actually she was glad to let Stacey wait on the poker-faced rancher.

After going out to the rest room for a quick freshening up, she went into the kitchen for a plate of food. Emerging with it minutes later, she found all the booths, including the rear one normally used by the staff, still occupied.

Two stools next to Dominick McCullough, however, had been vacated. Balancing her herb tea in one hand and the plate of chef salad as well as a bread plate with her roll and butter in the other, Beth hesitated over which stool to sit on.

Until Nick growled, "I don't bite, Elizabeth," and made her feel like a fool.

Chagrined, Beth set her meal down and sidled into the spot next to him. His shoulder, made even bulkier by the sheepskin jacket, intruded into her space. His sleeve rubbed her shoulder with every motion either of them made, and there was nowhere for her to move on the foot-wide, backless round stool that was bolted to the floor.

So she did what she could to ignore the contact and the man as she reached for a napkin and prepared to eat.

"Stuff like that'll never put meat on your bones," came another growl from her right. Her startled sideways glance caught him disdainfully eyeing her plate. "You oughta eat beef, and plenty of it...."

"Spoken like a true rancher," Beth quipped, forgetting for a moment that the man made her nervous. She nodded toward the mug he was cradling between large, workman's hands. "And you shouldn't drink so much coffee."

Surprise at her pert reply had Nick shifting for a better look at her. Her cheeks had turned a becoming pink and she kept her eyes determinedly fixed on her plate of rabbit food, giving him leisure to study her profile.

She had a nose like a miniature ski jump, he decided. And a luxuriant sweep of lashes shaded her downcast eyes. They were three shades darker than the brown mop of hair that she'd pinned away from her face with no apparent mind for style. Full lips were kept decorously closed as she chewed.

He wondered if her eyes were still sad and found that they were when at last she reacted to his intense regard and slanted him a glance. But he was intrigued to see something else there, too, just then. A spark of animation, almost of mischief brightened and beautified her features nearly as much as her smile for the cook had done earlier.

"Name's Nick McCullough, ma'am," he said, catching that furtive glance of hers and holding it. "And what might you be drinking there? Dishwater?"

The spark in her eyes intensified, and Nick felt ridiculously rewarded.

"Chamomile tea."

He'd noticed before that her voice was easy on the ear. Her precise enunciation prompted him to impulsively ask, "You're not from around here, are you?"

Only to immediately wish he'd kept his mouth shut when the lights in her eyes abruptly went out and she averted her face.

Ticked with himself, Nick stiffly shifted front and center again and went back to scowling into his coffee.

"Didn't mean to offend you, ma'am," he growled after a stretch of heavy silence during which he watched out of the corner of his eye, as she picked at her greens.

"You didn't really," she said, surprising him. And their eyes once again met. Hers still lacked the earlier animation, but steadily stayed on his. "My name's Beth Coleman. And you're right. I'm not from around here. I'm originally from San Francisco."

Beth figured it was safe enough to let that much about herself be known since her parents had moved to Boston from there shortly after her birth.

"That's all right." She cut off the protestation Nick was about to make. "It's no secret."

The way she said that made Nick think that other things about her probably were. He wondered what someone as wholesome and innocent looking as Elizabeth Coleman could possibly have to hide.

"Born right here, myself," he offered, not stopping to analyze why. Nedda and others who knew him would have been shocked to hear him open up to a stranger—a woman—like that. But he didn't stop to consider that, either.

He was busy being fascinated by the teasing glints that once again enlivened her gaze for just a blink as she asked, "Right here at Nedda's?"

He narrowed his eyes in reprimand, but couldn't restrain a small smile. "A bit of a smart aleck, aren't you?"

"Sorry."

But she didn't mean it and he liked that, too, deciding she must have been quite a little imp in her time. Until somebody...what? Walloped it out of her?

Nick was shocked by the murderous rage that notion aroused in him. It must have shown on his face, too, because Beth turned white as a ghost and jerked away from him when he went to lay a soothing hand on her arm.

"Whoa," he said in the same tone he'd use to soothe a skittish mare. "Easy now, li'l Betsy..."

Eyes wide with remnants of apprehension, she looked at him long and hard. And to Nick's overwhelming relief, visibly relaxed.

"Beth," she said, her voice even huskier than before. "Not Betsy."

Nick continued to meet her searching gaze. "I stand corrected, *Beth.*"

"It was my grandmother's name."

Nick took her offering of this bit of information as some sort of vote of confidence and was touched by it. "It's a nice one. But I like Elizabeth even better."

"Warm up your coffee, Nick?" Stacy was in front of them, brandishing a carafe.

"Ah, no thanks." Nick shot the waitress a quick, absent smile, eager for her to be gone so he could continue talking to Beth. But when he turned his attention back to her, she was concentrating on her salad in a way that said the conversation was over.

After watching her eat for another minute during which Nick could think of no diplomatic way to ask her all the things about herself he'd have liked to know—things such as: Who the hell are you? What brought you here? Are you planning to stay? What is it about you...?—he slapped a dollar bill onto the counter and hoisted himself up off the stool.

"I gotta get goin'," he muttered, tugging the brim of his hat low over his brow. "Pleasure talkin' to you."

Glancing up—somehow unable not to—Beth frowningly watched Nick McCullough's tall, broad form stalk out of the diner with just that bit of a limp. She was disturbed by the feeling of security he seemed to be taking away with him. For a few minutes here, his imposing presence had removed the sense of imminent threat that, awake or asleep, shrouded her very existence and made her view the world through a gray curtain of fear and suspicion. With him next to her, she'd forgotten all about being wary for a little while. She'd been ready—no, eager—to talk to him, almost to confide in him. Except for that moment when he'd looked so frighteningly fierce....

Why *had* he looked so fierce?

Though his velvet-soft words of reassurance had eased her instinctive reaction of alarm, Beth couldn't help but think she had somehow been the catalyst to the rage she'd briefly sensed in him.

Could it be he felt the same inexplicable tug of attraction she did, and—again like her—resented and feared it?

* * *

The parcel was nearly as big as she was; Beth's arms barely spanned its sides, making her grip on it tenuous. Staggering with it to the Starville post office—two walls of postal boxes divided by a counter—Beth hoped anyone she met would have the sense to step out of the way since she couldn't see a thing from behind her burden. She kept having to stop every few steps and balance the box on one raised knee while her hands tried to find renewed purchase on the smooth cardboard. Thank God she lived only a block up and across the street.

Standing on one leg like a wobbly crane, Beth supported the box and tried once again to get a good enough grip to make it all the way inside the post office building.

"Here, I'll get that door for you."

"Thanks very much."

Beth was silently blessing the unseen, kindly female voice when her burden suddenly vanished as if it had grown wings, to reveal a sheepskin-coated bulk that gruffly said, "Why don't *I* take that box?"

Swiftly raising her eyes several more inches, Beth encountered a similarly gruff, but no longer unfamiliar, visage daring her to find fault of some kind with his gallant gesture. Her arms and hands cramped and quivering, Beth wouldn't have dreamed of it.

Instead, she murmured her thanks and gratefully stepped through the door Nick McCullough's broad back was keeping ajar.

Nick followed her in and set the box on the counter.

"Thank you, Mr. McCullough."

"You're welcome, ma'am." Mindful of how awkwardly their last encounter at the diner had ended, Nick touched the brim of his hat and went to do what he'd come for—to check his box for mail.

The only other patron—the woman who'd offered to get the door for Beth—had been taken care of and it was Beth's turn next.

Nick heard Mariah, Starville's grizzled, but ever-cheerful postmistress, say, "Howdy, Miz Coleman. Sendin' a package today?"

Taking his time unlocking his box, Nick grimaced wryly at the question's inanity.

Beth's mellow alto held no amusement, only strain, however, when she answered, "That's right, Mrs. Daniels. I hope it won't cost an arm and a leg in postage."

"Well, let's see now. Brockton, Vermont...hmm. Pretty country around there, I've heard."

"Hmm."

"Kinda hilly and woodsy, right?"

"Ah, yes. That's right."

Beth sounded reluctant, Nick was not surprised to note. By now he'd gotten the distinct impression that she didn't like to talk about herself much.

Wanting to learn every little bit about her he could, Nick ignored the little voice that said he shouldn't be listening and took his time flipping through his stack of letters and junk mail so he could eavesdrop.

"Christmas presents?" Mariah was asking.

"Uh-huh." Beth was making a production out of digging her wallet out of a large leather shoulder bag.

"Got family there, do you?"

Nick caught himself holding his breath, only to release it with a ridiculous sense of disappointment when Beth evasively and vaguely replied, "Ah...sort of. More of a friend, actually."

"Well, ma'am..." Mariah's chuckle rumbled through her words like a herd of cattle across the range. "This friend o' your's present's gonna cost you eight-seventy-five parcel post."

"Will it get there in time for Christmas?"

"With more'n three weeks to go?" Mariah slapped on a metered strip of postage, wheezing asthmatically as she hoisted the package into a nearby bin. "I'm just sure your Jason Christofferson won't be disappointed."

"Thank you," Beth said, a little somberly to Nick's straining ear. *Jason Christofferson,* he thought. A friend of hers she'd called him. A lover...?

Annoyed with himself, Nick slammed shut his postal box and got himself to the door just in time to be able to reach around Beth and open it for her. The gesture brought them into close proximity; Beth's shoulder brushed the front of his jacket as she walked past. The top of her head passed just beneath his nose, leaving him with a tantalizing lungful of spring flowers, the scent of her shampoo.

"Thank you," she said, in much the same reservedly polite tone she'd used with the postmistress. The glance she slanted him clearly said, I can open my own door when my hands are free.

Just feeling a mite cantankerous? Nick wondered, or was she—heaven forbid—one of those radical women's libbers?

He glanced at her sharply and it hit him with a belated sense of shock that she was looking nothing at all like her usual self.

Not, he conceded, that he had any clear idea of what her usual self was, aside from the one he had—barely—come to know at the diner. There she always wore one of those tacky uniforms the color of Pepto-Bismol that

Nedda liked on her waitresses. And her hair was always nailed into place with all those metal pins.

Her hair. The smell of it still teased Nick's nostrils. The way she wore it today, without the pins, it was full and shiny. It framed Beth's face in a sleek, swingy page boy that didn't quite reach the shoulders of the short leather jacket she had on with faded blue jeans. The latter fit her so well, Nick's eyes about popped out as, narrow-hipped and long-legged, she walked ahead of him out onto the sidewalk.

At the diner, in her waitress persona, Beth Coleman had been a pleasant-looking woman whose big, sad eyes had struck an empathetic chord.

But here, now, dressed and groomed to a shine and distractedly tugging soft-as-butter kid gloves over her fingers, she was a picture right out of one of those women's magazines at Mueller's Mercantile.

Nick found that this version of Elizabeth Coleman struck a chord in him, too, but empathy had nothing whatever to do with it. Hormones had.

"Ahem..." He cleared a throat that had gone all tight and scratchy with pure male reaction. "Well. Can I walk you somewhere, uh, Beth?"

Somehow it was harder, too, to address *this* Elizabeth so familiarly by her first name. She looked so remote, out here with him now, so citified and... There was no other word for it. *Classy.*

And it struck him even more forcefully then that this was no ordinary waitress, this woman who'd drifted into his town, his life. This woman he should probably avoid but found himself seeking out at every opportunity. This woman who he'd bet had known the kind of life he and the good folks of Starville could only read about in magazines or watch on TV. A life of glamour, wealth and privilege. The good life.

What was it they called it? Life in the fast lane....

So what was she doing here, in a town where there were no lanes at all?

No fast lane, no slow lane, just one oiled strip of gravel road that divided the scattering of farm and ranch-oriented businesses from the scattering of residential houses, one school and one church. Just one country road in a town that still had wooden sidewalks.

Why was she here? And why did she have to be the one to stir him when so many others had not?

Nick didn't know and just then, drinking in the coolly elegant sight of her, really couldn't bring himself to care.

"I'm sorry, Mr. McCullough." Gloves on, she looked at him. Her features seemed tired and strained in the faltering early-December afternoon light. "You were saying...?"

Nick caught himself wanting to reach out and smooth the small frown from between her finely etched brows. "Name's Nick," he said gruffly. "I was wondering if maybe there was anything else I could do for you?"

"Oh."

Her smile was wan, distracted. As if she were too preoccupied to really take note of him. It rankled.

"No, thank you," she said. "I'm just going to stop at Mueller's for a couple of things...."

"Why, I'm headed there myself," Nick said smartly, though he hadn't been. In fact, the ranch pickup was parked by the feed store at the other end of town. But he wasn't used to women—or anyone—looking through him as if he weren't there. The McCulloughs in general, and himself in particular, were persons of consequence in these parts.

Besides which, though he wasn't a vain man or a man with a ravenous sense of self-importance, this was one woman he really wanted to be noticed by. "Mind if I walk along?"

"Would it matter if I did?"

Ah, but Nick liked those fiery salvos she occasionally let loose. His lips twitched as he fell into step beside her.

"I wouldn't want to impose," he modestly told her. And knew from the sharp look she slanted him that she hadn't missed the little arrow he'd shot, but merely didn't deign to fire back.

"Think it'll snow soon?" he asked, after they'd walked awhile in silence.

Another narrowed glance flashed his way. This one held a definite gleam of humor. Though she made no reply, Nick felt vastly heartened.

A group of teenagers was coming toward them, pushing and shoving each other and hogging the sidewalk. Nick took Beth's arm to steer her out of their path, an instinctive gesture of courtesy toward a woman, as inbred in him as breathing.

He was therefore unprepared for, and not a little taken aback by, Beth's almost violent reaction. Flinching as if he'd hurt her, she jerked away from him.

"Don't—"

The word came out in a voice etched with hysteria. She closed her eyes and cut it off with a shuddering inhalation.

"Don't...touch me," she said in a quieter tone though Nick could still see panic lurking in eyes that were wide and golden-green with alarm. "P-please..."

Nick was thunderstruck, and without a clue as to how to act or what to say. His bemusement must have shown because Beth's expression suddenly became a study in mortified apology.

"I'm sorry," she murmured. "Please. You didn't do anything. It wasn't you. It—I—" She briefly touched her forehead with a visibly trembling hand. "I'm sorry."

They stared at each other, Nick trying to understand, and Beth silently, helpless—or unwilling—to elaborate or explain.

Nick cleared his throat. "If you ever want to talk about it..."

"It wouldn't do any good."

"Never know till you try it."

"I *have* tried it. But, thank you, Mr. McCullough." He saw her try for a smile and give up. "Please excuse me."

Brushing past him, Beth hurried across the street, leaving Nick to frown after her in consternation until she'd disappeared inside Myrna Stiller's rooming house.

Chapter Three

Beth raced up the two flights of stairs to her room as if a pack of dogs were at her heels and ready to eat her for supper. Her breath came in labored gasps as she slammed the door shut and, still gripping the handle, turned and subsided against it. Her legs shook; her insides fluttered as if a swarm of locusts had taken wing there. She was slowly rolling her head from side to side, her eyes closed.

Oh, how she hated what she'd done out on that sidewalk. How she had acted. *Re*acted! For a moment out there she had lost it. And all because a man had put his hand on her, though the touch had been nothing more than a gesture of courteous concern.

Chivalry is still alive and well in Starville, Washington, Beth thought half-hysterically. Not every man's touch is a threat or a prelude to violence....

Oh, God! Beth buried her face in her hands. It hadn't just been Dominick McCullough's hand on her that had set her off. It was everything. Everything! Jason's letter yesterday, the presents she'd so lovingly wrapped and packaged last night, and had mailed today. The knowledge that J.C. would be out on the streets again in just two more weeks and the promise he'd made her. The promise she didn't doubt for a second he had every intention of keeping.

It had all caught up with her out there on that street with that rancher.

Beth's hands fell listlessly to her sides as she pushed away from the door and with dragging steps crossed over to the window. It faced Starville's main street. Just over to the right half a block was where she had turned on Dominick McCullough like a woman possessed.

Which she was, of course. Had been, for the past twelve years. Possessed by the devil himself come to life in the guise of friend, lover, husband...

Ex-husband.

Semantics.

You'll never get away from me, Liz. I'll kill you first....

He'd tried. And he would try again.

Beth's lips twisted in a humorless smile as she scanned the street. Poor rancher. Poor Dominick McCullough. He'd been so shocked by her reaction, she half expected him to still be standing there trying to make sense of what had transpired.

He wasn't, of course. He'd gotten himself out of there, no doubt berating himself for ever having given a crazy woman like her the time of day. And not about to repeat that mistake anytime soon.

Not that it wouldn't be better that way, Beth realized. It would. For both of them. In spite of everything she'd been through, she was still woman enough to sense that this man, this rancher, was more than superficially interested in her. What was more, she was even still woman enough to be flattered, to be warmed by his interest.

Which had to be the only reason why knowing he would drop her like a hot coal after this was causing her this twinge of regret. Almost of pain. For a short little while there, Nick McCullough had made her feel like a whole woman again, a *normal* woman, even when she'd known damn good and well she wasn't either of those anymore.

And now he knew it, too.

During the following week, Nick McCullough came into the diner every day, usually at the tail end of the lunch hour. He always sat at the counter. Those times when Beth would be the one waiting on him, they talked sparingly of inconsequential stuff. Like polite strangers everywhere, they'd say things such as: would it snow, or wasn't it turning cold, or how did Nick like his eggs, or steak or whatever it was he was having. When Beth went on break, she made sure she sat in the back booth.

She did nothing to encourage Nick. As, indeed, *he* did nothing overt that might suggest he was looking for, or would welcome encouragement. Except that he came into the diner every day.

His regular arrivals were causing Nedda and the rest of the staff to start exchanging meaningful glances and digs in the ribs.

"My goodness, Nick," Nedda exclaimed when he walked in again that Thursday. "Did Jeanie Mulligan take sick, you don't get fed at home anymore? Not that I don't appreciate the business, mind you," she hastened to add.

"Jeanie's fine," was all Nick replied, seeing no reason to explain himself. "I'll have a burger today, Elizabeth."

"Coffee, Mr. McCullough?"

"That'd be fine." After that one time out on the sidewalk, Nick hadn't invited Beth to use his given name again. Not that he didn't want her to, he did. What he didn't want was to be rebuffed again, no matter how obliquely.

Beth poured him a cup. "That's some wind out there today, isn't it?"

"Sure is. Colder'n Hades, too."

"Hades would be hot, I expect, Mr. McCullough."

Nick choked on his sip of coffee. Damn, but she'd done it again. For the first time since—

He worked at a scowl, but his heart felt lighter than it had all week. "There you go again, being a smart aleck."

When he caught her little smirk, he had to grin. And admit to himself that it was the hope of catching these little glimpses of who she once must have been that kept luring him back to Nedda's for more.

It sure's hell wasn't the coffee. It tasted sicklier today than Beth's funny weed tea had looked. "Hell, Nedda, I can see the bottom of this cup. What'd you do, run out of coffee?"

"Not ever'body likes to drink tar, Nick," was Nedda's unshaken reply. "Beth. He wants it stronger, whyn't you add a spoonful of instant to it."

"Instant?" Horrified, Nick clapped a hand over his cup. "Don't even think about it."

Beth brought him his burger plate. "Here you go, Mr. McCullough. Anything else I can do for you?"

You can sit down and talk to me. "No, I guess this'll do it, thanks."

"Enjoy."

He didn't. Because when Beth went on break, she went to the rest room, got her food and joined that damned Charley in that back booth of theirs. Again.

Leaving most of his burger uneaten, Nick slapped down some bills and stalked out of the diner.

Everybody's gaze flew to Beth.

Darling Jason,

Thank you for your letter. I've read it six times since it came. I love you so much. I miss you all the

Nooohhh...!

At her wits' end and ready to tear out her hair, Beth reduced the sheet of stationery to shreds. Just like she'd done with the half dozen others before it. Dammit, what're you doing writing such garbage? she railed. The last thing your son needs from you is this weepy, self-pitying—

Ooh!

Needing space, needing air, needing to *scream* out her anguish and frustration, Beth grabbed a coat and ran from the room. Stuffing her arms into sleeves, clumsy with agitation, she clattered down the stairs.

Bursting out onto the sidewalk, she didn't slow down. Head lowered against a mean northerly wind, hands stuffed into the pockets of her long cashmere coat, she blindly marched down Main Street.

Her thoughts were a riot of self-recrimination and self-loathing. It was her own fault she was in this mess. Her child needed to be with her. *She* needed to be with her child. And yet there was an entire continent between them keeping them apart.

She was afraid to go to him. She was afraid *not* to go to him. She wished she could bring him here. She knew it wasn't *possible* to bring him here. It wasn't safe. Not yet.

Would they always have to hide? Would they ever be safe?

Oh God, would they *ever* be safe?

"Beth!"

The call of her name brought Beth up short. She looked around in confusion to discover that there was no longer any town around her. There was only a cold and dark country road.

And a man's voice calling, "Elizabeth Coleman, what in *hell* do you think you're doing way out here in this weather at this time o'night?"

Nick McCullough had pulled his ranch pickup to an idling stop alongside of her; the truck's headlights illuminated a slice of rolling range and fallow fields abutting the road. And utter darkness.

Beth was in no mood for company. Even this man's. *Especially* this man's.

She rounded on him. "Don't you have a home to go to?"

He had the nerve to chuckle. "I'm headed there now. And you oughta do the same."

"When I'm good and ready, I will! I'm a grown woman, Mr. McCullough...."

"Believe me, I've noticed," Nick muttered sourly, reaching across the cab to throw open the passenger door. "Get in. I'll drive you back."

Beth made no move to accept his invitation. "When I want to go back, I'll get myself back, Mr. McCullough. On foot."

"All right." For a man with a limp, and no longer young, he was amazingly quick. He'd killed the engine, slid out of the truck and was standing in front of Beth in just the blink of an eye. He slammed the passenger door shut. "You want to walk? We'll walk."

"We?"

"That's what I said."

He turned up the collar of his sheepskin jacket, stuck his hands in his pockets and started out. Beth was so dumbfounded, for a moment she could only stare.

"But I want to walk alone!" she finally called after him, her voice pretty close to a wail. "Go home!"

"Not until you do!" came Nick's unperturbed reply.

Which was when she lost it again. Gripping her head, her eyes on the stars, her voice breaking, she yelled, "But I no longer *have* a home! Can't you understand that? There isn't anywhere—"

"Yes, there *is.*" Nick was back in front of her, pulling her hands away from her head. "Elizabeth. Look at me."

Eyes burning with unshed tears, Beth reluctantly did as he asked.

"If there's anything I can do, I want you to know you've only got to ask."

Beth was shaking her head. "There isn't anything."

"Come into the truck." Ignoring her resistance, Nick coaxed her toward the vehicle. "There is a roadhouse up a ways, a tavern. Let me take you there, buy you a drink."

"I don't want a drink."

"It doesn't have to be alcohol, Beth. Have some coffee, or some of that whatchamacallit tea you like. We can talk...."

"I don't want to talk." Which wasn't true. She wanted, needed, desperately to talk to someone. To share her burden. To let go, just for a little while. But afraid to trust, Beth locked her knees against his attempts to steer her toward the pickup. Shaking off his guiding hand, she averted her face.

"Elizabeth." Nick gently coaxed her chin around with a callused finger. "Like I told you once before, I don't mean to impose. If you really want me to leave you alone, say so now and I'll never bother you again."

With his fingers still holding her chin, there was no way Beth could avoid looking into his eyes. The quiet steadiness of his gaze on hers was mesmerizing. His very presence reassured.

How tall he was, quite a bit taller than she. How wide his shoulders; the breadth of them blocked the darkness behind him from view. The bulk of him, his steady regard, the lines etched around his mouth and eyes—everything about Nick McCullough spoke of steadfast, rock-hard maturity. It spoke of character, and of a life that hadn't spared him his full share of pain and loneliness.

It spoke of pride. Pride that would not allow him to extend a hand to Beth again if she pushed it away now.

It had been so long since there'd been someone strong for Beth to lean on, someone decent and caring. Not since her grandfather Coleman had died.

Ten years already. Oh, Grampa...

You had such high hopes for your little girl. You were so proud of me on my wedding day. Your beautiful princess you called me. And J.C. was my Prince Charming....

Only he wasn't, Grampa. Do you hear me? He wasn't what you and I thought he was.

Is anybody?

There is no way of knowing until it's too late.

Exactly, Beth thought, and stepped out of reach of Nick's rough-gentle touch. "It's good of you to concern yourself, Mr. McCullough, but..."

After that moment when he'd sensed her careful guard slipping, Beth's renewed withdrawal was like a slap in the face. Nick spat a harsh expletive which she ignored.

"I'm fine," she said, stiffly. "Really. And if it'll make you feel any better, I'll turn around right now and—"

"Dammit," Nick exploded. "This isn't about me feelin' better, it's about *you!*"

"You're shouting at me."

"Because you're the most mule-headed female I've ever met!"

"Well, what do you want from me?" Beth's voice, too, was climbing up there. "Why can't you just leave me alone?"

"Because..." Nick started, but then, at a loss for a rational reply, threw up his hands and didn't say any more.

Which left them to glare at each other in agitated silence, breathing as hard as if they'd been running a race and were now facing each other at the finish line.

But then, up until that moment, each of them *had* been doing their share of running, hadn't they? And in the same direction, too.

Away from pain, and from anything, any*one,* who might cause more of it. Away from friendship, and solace, and understanding because there was risk in accepting them. Away from life.

The risk of getting hurt again had kept each of them running until eventually, somehow, they'd both arrived... here.

A man and a woman facing each other on a country road that stretched cold and endless into darkness, much as their lives would continue to do unless they allowed themselves to reach out just one more time. To trust just one more time. To become vulnerable to pain just one more time.

To pain, yes—but also to joy, and companionship, and maybe, just maybe...

Nick deeply inhaled. Very carefully so as not to frighten her, he laid his hands on Beth's shoulders. When she didn't flinch, he tightened his grip just a little. Just enough to emphasize what he was about to say.

"I've been alone a long time, Elizabeth. Though there's people all around here who're my family and friends, I've been alone in all the ways that count. It was what I wanted. What I needed."

He brought his face closer. Beth could see every line there, every wrinkle that life and the elements had placed there. But she also recognized and responded to the emotional intensity that made his voice harsh and his hands tighten once more. "But I don't think that's what *you* want and need, Elizabeth. Is it?"

His eyes riveted hers. Though she couldn't discern their color out here in the dark of night, she knew them to be blue as a summer sky, and just now they seemed able to see into her very soul. How else could he have known...?

Beth shook her head. "No. It isn't."

Nick released her and moved toward the truck. "Come on. Let me drive you home."

Home. The prospect of being cooped up in her little dormer alone with her thoughts, with no one to talk to, with no TV and too tied up in knots to be able to read, didn't bear contemplating. An hour or so among people, on the other hand...

"Is that offer of a drink still open?"

* * *

Starkey's was a noisy, dim, peanut-shells-on-the-floor kind of place. It was unlike any drinking establishment Beth had ever set foot in. Not that there'd been that many.

A massive, ornately carved bar fronted a wall of bottles against a mirrored background. There were no bar stools. Instead, a scuffed and pitted, no-longer-shiny brass foot rail provided ease of sorts to the booted patrons in cowboy hats or ball caps, faded plaid flannel and jeans who slouched shoulder-to-shoulder along the bar. They were nursing beers or shots of stronger stuff, arguing and knocking the government, women, their bosses in a rough cacophony of male voices punctuated by occasional bursts of raucous laughter.

There were only a few women, and they were dressed pretty much the same way as the men they were with. They sat in the collection of booths that lined two walls, or at little tables around the littered square of a dance floor that fronted a now vacant bandstand.

From a jukebox, Willie Nelson bewailed the loss of his woman.

"There's dancing here tomorrow," Nick said, lightly touching the small of her back to usher Beth toward a booth. "Every Friday and Saturday night, for that matter."

"Do you come here often?"

"No." Helping Beth out of her coat, Nick noted the quality of it. Unlike some others in Starville, he did know the feel and cost of cashmere and, slanting Beth a quick, assessing glance, couldn't help but wonder yet again what quirk of fate had brought someone like her out here to the boonies. It clearly wasn't her usual stomping ground.

Watching her slide into the booth, shapely and elegant in a fine wool sweater and jeans that weren't intended for work like everybody else's around here, Nick tried to calculate what the odds might be of her staying for more than a few short weeks or months. Mighty slim, he'd bet. And found himself wondering what it would take to better those odds.

There's no fool like an old fool.

Nick shrugged out of his own coat and, hanging it next to Beth's on the pegs provided at each booth, the set of his lips tightened even more. Because if anything could have more glaringly underscored the disparity between his natural environment and Beth's than the sight of his battered sheepskin rubbing up to the refined elegance and lushness of her wool, he didn't know what.

Grimly, Nick yanked off his hat, slapped it on top of the coats and sat down.

He was raking both hands through his hat-flattened hair when a waitress in boots and tassels plunked down a basket of unshelled peanuts, spilling some in the process. "What'll ya have, folks?"

"Elizabeth?"

"A glass of Chardonnay would be nice."

The waitress stopped chewing her gum long enough to give Beth a blank stare. "A glass of what, hon?"

"Dry white wine," Nick supplied with an unreadable glance at Beth who was visibly disconcerted. "A beer for me."

"We have—"

"Whatever's on tap's fine. Thanks."

Aware that for some reason Nick seemed to have withdrawn into himself, Beth bit her lip. She picked up the cocktail napkin the waitress had put in front of her and absently shredded it as she scanned the room with assumed casualness. She was angry with herself for having broken the vow she'd made. The vow to keep away from even superficial involvements.

If you didn't make friends, didn't form attachments, then leaving wouldn't hurt nearly so much, if and when it became necessary to leave.

Beth propped her elbows on the table and laced her hands together imagining how it might be if it wouldn't become necessary. Starville would be a great community in which to raise her son. She'd give up her job at Nedda's and maybe dust off her teaching degree. Maybe open that preschool she'd always dreamed about.

Once things became normal...

Beth pressed her lips against her hands and closed her eyes, knowing there would never be that kind of normal possible for her here in Starville. Indeed, not even in this country, as long as J. C. Christofferson was bent on revenge.

No, best stick with her plan to save her money and take Jason to Canada. Six months. If she could only stay hidden from J.C. for six more months, she'd have it made.

Six more months without Jason...

"Beth, are you all right?"

It was Nick, gruffly asking. He'd just realized what an ass he was being, sitting there grimly brooding about the differences in their coats, and what that implied, after he'd all but browbeaten Beth into coming here with him.

Opening her eyes, Beth gave him a smile that matched her tremulous sigh. "I guess. Just not very good company, I'm afraid."

"I didn't bring you here to be entertained."

"Why exactly *did* you bring me, Mr. McCullough?"

"Nick."

"Why do you even bother with me?"

"I bother because I like you."

"You don't know me well enough to like me," Beth argued, though Nick's words and steady regard warmed her as nothing had in a long, long time.

"Don't I?"

The waitress brought their drinks. They each took their glass and, gazes locked, raised them to their lips. Beth sipped and, breaking the eye contact that had suddenly become vaguely disturbing, carefully set her glass down.

Nick took another healthy swallow. Beth looked back at him and watched the movement of his Adam's apple. She felt her palms grow damp.

"How's the wine?" Nick asked.

"Mmm, good."

Their gazes met and meshed once again. Beth's heart did a funny little flutter that reverberated through her stomach and lower.

Searching for something to say that would keep the conversation light, she voiced the first thing that popped into her head. "I just realized that I've never seen more than just a fringe of your hair before. It's nice."

At her words, Nick once again plunged both hands into the dark, graying fullness, causing chaos instead of order. "I need to get it cut."

"Uh-uh." The big man's obvious self-consciousness charmed Beth and restored the rest of her poise. "I like it fine the way it is."

Which was true. Beth found the way that salt-and-pepper thickness touched the back of Nick's shirt collar very attractive. Not that the rest of him was hard on the eyes. Quite the contrary. Nick McCullough was the archetypal cowboy. Proud and straight, lean of hip and wide of shoulder, with features on which life's hardships, as well as years of working out-of-doors, had left their signature.

Squint lines, character lines, lines caused less by laughter than by sorrow—together they created a face stamped by strength and courage and forthrightness. Beth found it undeniably attractive.

And she thought, Now why couldn't someone like Nick McCullough have found me before J. C. Christofferson did? I'll bet he'd never—

She cut the thought short with a resolute squaring of the shoulders and took another stab at conversation.

"Nedda tells me you're not up for grabs, Nick," she said. "Her choice of words, by the way. So, uh, are you married?"

Nick shook his head. "No, I'm not."

He looked into his beer, then screwed his eyes back up to hers. "How 'bout you?"

"No," Beth said quietly, but Nick didn't miss the way she touched her ring finger with her thumb.

"I'm a widower," he offered. But if he was hoping for elucidation from Beth in return, he was disappointed.

"I'm sorry" was all she said.

"It's been a while," Nick said gruffly. "Five years."

"What happened?" Beth asked, only to immediately take the question back. "I'm sorry, I don't mean to pry."

"That's okay. It's no secret."

"You haven't wanted to marry again?"

"Hell, no."

Though the words came straight from the heart, Nick couldn't believe he'd spoken them out loud. Chagrined, he saw that, obviously, neither could Beth. She looked taken aback, to say the least.

He never talked about his marriage except in the most general terms and really didn't want to explain now, either. But he did. "We hadn't been happy for a long time."

Beth bit her lip. She could understand about unhappiness, but mourned what Nick's words once more brought home to her: Happily ever after was a myth. "I'm sorry. . . ."

Nick would just as soon have left it there, but her softly voiced sympathy seemed to have uncorked all the stuff he'd kept bottled up for so long.

"I wanted children. Susan didn't."

Beth nodded, remembering how excited she'd been to find out she was pregnant with Jason. And how livid J.C.

"We fought about it a lot."

Again Beth nodded, and hoped the empathy she felt for Nick showed on her face. She took another sip of her wine and prepared to hear him out. Clearly, Nick needed someone to talk to every bit as much as she did. Maybe more.

With an encouraging smile, she prepared to listen, ready for anything. For anything but what he said.

"I killed her, you know."

Chapter Four

For a moment, Beth didn't think she'd heard him right. But when Nick raised his eyes from the contemplation of his beer, their bleak expression dispelled that notion.

Beth didn't know what her own expression showed. She'd never been very good at dissembling, and she was a mass of confused reaction inside. Shock, horror, disbelief. Most of all, disbelief. She might not be the best judge of character where men were concerned— Lord, she was probably the *worst*—but she knew with unshakable conviction that this man, that Dominick McCullough, was no more capable of murder than she was.

"What happened?" she asked quietly.

He hesitated, closing his eyes a moment. "We'd flown to Coeur D'Alene to meet some friends from the East Coast who were vacationing there," he finally said, his voice low. "I still owned a plane in those days. A Cessna. They don't build 'em anymore. Flying back, we hit one of those freak summer thunderstorms we're prone to around here...."

Nick's lips twisted and he stared into his beer again for a long while.

Beth, watching him with her heart in her throat, wanted to reach out to him, but something about the set of his shoulders, the grim working of his jaw, told her it would be best to let him be. It was obvious he was reliving the incident and struggling to give voice to undoubtedly painful images and recollections.

"We got hit by lightning. The plane dropped like a bomb. Somehow I managed to get out," he said without looking up. "Or maybe by some miracle I was thrown clear. I don't remember. That's the hell of it."

His tortured gaze surged back to hers. "Not remembering. All I knew, when I woke up in the hospital, was that I was alive and Susan was dead."

His voice dropped to a mere whisper. "And all I could think about was that now I'd *never* have that son—*Damn.*"

He covered his eyes, then slowly scraped the hand down the length of his face and over his mouth before letting it drop to the table.

"I've never told this to a living soul," he said awkwardly. The confession had cost him. He felt vulnerable, naked. Defenseless. The feelings didn't sit well and so he added, almost with belligerence, "Don't know what the hell got into me, bending your ears like that."

"Maybe it was time you told somebody," Beth said. "Maybe it was time you laid it all to rest, time you gave yourself a break. What happened was clearly an accident. A horrible, freakish accident that you could only have avoided if you'd never left the ground."

"I got the weather report before we took off. If I'd thought for a minute—"

"Nick." Beth leaned toward him for emphasis. "It wasn't your fault."

"Yeah, I know. I know." His lips compressed. "In any case, I haven't piloted a plane since. Doubt I ever will again."

"I guess I can understand how that would be."

"Really?"

Beth absently watched her fingers toy with her glass. "Hmm."

"You've been married, too, haven't you?"

His quiet question abruptly froze Beth's fingers and brought her head up sharply.

Their eyes met. Hers held a hint of what? Panic? Nick kept his thoughts to himself and said, "You want to talk about it?"

"No!" Beneath his steady regard, Beth faltered. "I mean there's nothing to talk *about.*"

No way was she going to admit to this man why and how her marriage had failed. Her pain was her own, just as it always had been. During all those years of unhappiness and abuse, none of their friends, their family—*nobody*—had ever been the wiser. To the world, theirs had been the ideal marriage, with herself the eager helpmate and J.C. the adoring husband who showered his wife with costly gifts.

Nobody knew the price Beth had paid for those gifts. In terms of pain, both inside and out. In terms of shame, and degradation. And, finally, of self-loathing. The only thing she'd had to cling to in those days and since, was her pride. The pride that wouldn't allow her to talk of the hell in which she lived. The pride that, right or wrong, had kept her trapped in that hell, enduring, honoring the marriage vows she had uttered with such love and conviction. The pride that would probably still be keeping her trapped, if J.C. hadn't slapped Jason....

But even then she hadn't been able to bring herself to tell of her shame. She had found herself an attorney and she had talked to him. But not to anyone else. And she wouldn't, couldn't, talk to Dominick McCullough now.

Could she?

"Take it from one who only just learned this," Nick quietly told her. "Talking about it really does ease the load."

Beth bit her lip. To her horror, tears filled her throat and welled into her eyes. She knew that if she so much as blinked, they'd roll down her cheek. Widening her eyes, she averted her face, only to whip her head around again at Nick's quiet, "What ghosts are you running from, Elizabeth?"

Trapped by the force of Nick's gaze, she nevertheless said nothing.

"It's plain as day you don't belong here," he continued in the same quiet tone. "And that you're hurting. It's in your eyes. I knew it the first time I ever saw you. And then tonight. You were marching down that dark and lonely country road like you couldn't get away from something fast and far enough when all the time that pain of yours is running right along with you. Isn't that so, Elizabeth? Isn't it always there, beside you, the hell of it? The pain of it?"

Ignoring her silent protest, the denying shake of the head, he said, "Talk to me, Elizabeth. Trust me with whatever's making you so sad. I'd like to help if I could—"

"You can't." The words were little more than a choked whisper and she immediately repeated them more forcefully. "You can't."

"Try me," Nick said, undeterred. "Talk to me. What can it hurt?"

"Me." Suddenly angry, Beth glared at the man across from her. She knew he meant well, but why couldn't he leave well enough alone? Just because he'd bared his soul to her didn't mean she had to do the same.

"It would hurt *me,*" she repeated harshly. "So just leave it alone."

Keeping her gaze averted, she slid out of the booth. "I'd like to go now, please."

"You can't keep running forever, Elizabeth."

"Knowing what the alternative is?" Unaware of what she'd admitted with that grim question, her hands shaking, Beth tossed Nick his hat and yanked her coat off the peg next to his. "You bet I can."

Filled with frustration at not being able to keep her from shoring up those protective barriers again, Nick slammed his hat on his head and also got to his feet. Shrugging into his own coat, he somberly watched Beth do the same.

He was racking his brain for something to say when she looked up at him and spoke first. Her face red with embarrassment, she stiffly said, "I'm sorry, but it just occurred to me that I didn't bring any money. I'll have to owe you for the wine."

Nick's eyebrows arched. It was all he could do not to laugh, it seemed so incongruous that she'd stop to worry about something that was—to him—so picayune, given the intensity and seriousness of their discussion. But her chin was up, her fine eyes flared and the faint tremble of her lower lip bespoke an emotional turmoil that only fierce pride was holding in check. This mattered to her, and a show of amusement or the wrong word would surely make her snap.

So Nick only allowed a small smile to curl his lip. "Don't worry about it," he said mildly, dropping some bills on the table. "In these parts it's customary for a man to pay for his lady's drink."

The glance she shot him as she preceded him out the door was reassuring in that it told him her equilibrium had been restored.

"Thanks," she said. "But I'll pay you back just the same. After all, I'm not your lady."

Following her out to the truck, Nick was disconcerted by the notion that he'd like it a lot if she were.

The notion stuck with him and got stronger as he drove Beth home in relative silence, dropped her off at the rooming house and headed for the ranch. So much so, that he made a snap decision of the kind that sent Jeanie Mulligan, his housekeeper, into a tailspin.

"We're gonna have us a party, Jean," he came out of his office to casually inform her that Friday afternoon, just as if it hadn't been more than five years since there'd been any sort of entertaining done at the Triple Creek.

"You mean, as in havin' folks over 'n' all?" Jeanie asked incredulously.

"Yup." He straddled a kitchen chair and stole one of her fresh-baked cookies. "Nothin' fancy," he said, munching. "Just family, and a couple others. Thirty or so, I'd say." He snitched another cookie. "Hey, these're good."

"Yeah, and they're for after supper." Jean moved the plate out of reach. "So just when were you thinking of havin' this shindig, if you don't mind my asking?"

"Tomorrow night."

"Tomorrow night?" Jeanie gaped at him with her fists planted on comfortably ample hips. "You expect me to get this house and enough food for thirty people ready by tomorrow night? Nick McCullough, are you feelin' all right in the head?"

"Never better."

"Hell, and what's the occasion, if I might ask?"

Though as far as Nick was concerned the "occasion" was nothing but a ploy to get Beth Coleman out to his house in a sufficiently crowded social setting that wouldn't spook her, he had a reply all prepared.

"After nearly a hundred years, we finally got the land with the third creek on it," he told Jean, and everybody else who asked when he later called to invite them. "That makes the name of this ranch legitimate at last. Now if that ain't reason to celebrate, I don't know what is."

Armed with Jeanie's list of things to get, Nick headed into town soon afterward. He stopped at the diner to invite Nedda. And to talk to Beth.

It was the lull before supper. Beth was refilling salt and pepper shakers and catsup bottles before going off shift at four o'clock. Donna James, who worked part-time—the dinner shift after her husband came home from work to mind the kids—would shortly be arriving to relieve her.

Beth was tired. She hadn't slept much after her surprising evening with Nick McCullough and, except for her half-hour lunch break, she'd been on her feet since the diner had opened at seven that morning. It would be good to get off work, put her feet up and...do what? Stare at the walls and brood about Jason? Or stare at the pages of a book, unable to make sense out of even a single word because she was thinking of and pining for her son?

Beth neatly arranged the replenished containers of condiments and, sighing, gave the tabletop another half-hearted wipe before moving on to the next booth.

Someone had read a newspaper there and had left it. Its pages were haphazardly scrunched every which way and Beth picked it up section by section to smooth it out. It wasn't the weekly *Starville Gazette,* but the much larger and bulkier daily *Seattle Times* which some of the ranchers subscribed to by mail.

Absently, her mind on Jason and Christmas and the parcel she'd sent, Beth smoothed the want ads section on top of the arts and entertainment section and the stock market listings, and gathered up the sports section and folded it in half. As she did so, her gaze idly scanned the headlines, large and small, without consciously registering any of them. Until she saw the picture.

It was only a small photograph, the sort of publicity shot of their players that teams of every sport handed out to the press. It showed a man in hockey regalia, his face slightly battered beneath tousled black curls and a rakish grin and was inserted into a short column, headed Former NHL All-Star Released.

Beth's heart froze in her chest. Her horrified eyes read only the first line. "Ex-Chicago Black Hawks goalie, J. C. Christofferson, sentenced to eight months in prison for assault and harrassment—"

He was out. A whole week early!

Beth felt herself strangling and frantically swallowed. Her heart began beating again, but so fast, it made her dizzy. She was panicking, hyperventilating, as her mind kept screaming, He's out. He's out.

A surge of adrenaline activated the fight or flight reaction and, still clutching the paper, Beth blindly whirled and ran for the door.

Nick was just coming in when she plowed right into him.

"Whoa," he said, chuckling, making a grab to steady her. Only to have Beth wrench herself free with a wild-eyed stare and keep right on running.

Nick exchanged a startled glance with Nedda, then spun and charged after Beth as fast as his bum hip allowed.

Luckily there was no traffic, since neither one of them looked left or right before sprinting across the road. Beth was headed for the rooming house. All she could think was to get to her room and lock herself in.

He was out. J.C. was out. He was out and coming after her. And Jason...

I'll kill you, Liz! I get my hands on you, I'll kill you both!

Gasping for breath, Beth ran faster.

"Elizabeth!" Nick shouted, closing in on her despite his limp and the ache in his hip.

If Beth heard him, she gave no sign. She didn't slow. Through the front door she burst, up the stairs. At last she was at her door. Almost safe now. She turned the handle, pushed. And pushed.

From behind her came the sound of labored breathing as Nick raced up the stairs.

Frantic, Beth pushed again at her door. It was locked. Of course, it was locked. The key was back at the diner. In her coat pocket...

She pounded her fists against the door in helpless frustration and slumped, letting her forehead drop against the smooth wood just as Nick reached her.

Strangled sobs mixing with her gasps for air, Beth would have sagged to the floor had not strong arms reached out and caught her.

"Elizabeth," Nick said, panting, turning her toward him. "For God's sake, sweetheart, what's the matter?"

"Go away." Wildly tossing her head from side to side, Beth struggled against Nick's hold. Her fists, one of them still clutching the paper, beat weakly against his chest. "Go away. Leave me alone...."

"Now you know I can't do that, li'l Betsy." Nick spoke softly, tenderly, intent only on calming her. He pulled her more tightly against him, trapping her flailing arms between their bodies. "Hush, now," he murmured. "Be still now, darlin'. I've got you. It's okay."

Feeling the fight go out of her, he led her to the stairs and gently urged her down on the top step. "Sit here a minute now," he told her with a reassuring squeeze before he let go. "I'll get Myrna's spare key for you...."

"My purse... My coat..."

"They're fine. After a while I'll fetch 'em for you. Don't you worry, now. I'll be right back."

Beth sat unmoving on the top stair, as in a stupor. Her mind was as blank as the stare she directed into nothingness. Her heart no longer raced, but beat slowly, leadenly in her chest. J. C. Christofferson had been let out early....

Nick came back up the stairs. One of his legs brushed her shoulder as he stepped past her to unlock the door and she shivered. She was cold suddenly. So terribly cold.

Her teeth chattered as Nick urged her to her feet and into her room. He led her to the threadbare, drab-green overstuffed chair and urged her down into it. Taking the quilt off her bed, he wrapped it around her, all the time murmuring soothing bits of nonsense. Or, at least, they seemed like nonsense to Beth because nothing registered but the almost hypnotic quiet of his tone.

"Do you have any brandy?" Nick looked around her small quarters, appalled at the meagerness of her comforts but touched by the obvious efforts she'd made to make the place home. "Any whiskey or something?"

He poked through the shelves above and below the hot plate with no luck.

"There's some wine in the fridge," Beth roused herself sufficiently to say. "If you'd like some."

Nick's chuckle was grim. "It's not for me I'm asking, Elizabeth, but for you. I figure, a little shot of something would warm you up a bit."

"Oh, God, I couldn't." The thought of swallowing anything just then had nausea surging into Beth's throat.

"Well, all right then." Nick hunkered down in front of her and tugged on the newspaper. "If you'll let go of this, I'll rub your hands for you."

"No." Beth's eyes widened again in alarm and her grip on the paper tightened. "I've got to get away from here. I've got to get to Jason. Warn him..." She struggled to stand, to get out of the chair, but Nick blocked her with his body.

"Elizabeth." He caught her hands in one of his and urged her face around with the other. "It's over."

Beth struggled against his hold, but to no avail. His hands and eyes held her gently but relentlessly.

"Whatever it is, sweetheart, this is the end. Do you hear me? No more running. I'm here and you're safe. Trust me on that."

"You don't know what you're talking about."

"Then tell me, Elizabeth," he urged softly, stroking his thumb along her jaw and the downy curve of her cheek. "Let me help you, darlin'. Give it up...."

Beth looked into the honest blueness of Nick's eyes, saw the concern there, and slowly, slowly the icy grip of fear and horror melted and relaxed in response to it. And even though she knew there was nothing he could do to help in the long run, his stalwart presence here—*now*—was a comfort she sorely needed and didn't have the strength any longer to turn away from.

On a shivery breath she closed her eyes. "Here." She extended the paper. "It... It's all in there."

Frowning, Nick took the newspaper out of her hand. He shook it out and sat back on his heels, scanning the sports page without any idea of what he was looking for.

"Down at the bottom," Beth whispered tonelessly. "Right-hand side. The picture."

"Ah." Nick spotted it then. His eyes rapidly took in the header, the photo, the gist of the text. Christofferson... Where had he heard Beth mention that name before?

"This man, he's...?"

"My husband." Bone-weary, Beth let her head fall against the backrest and closed her eyes. She tucked up her legs and, on a renewed shiver, pulled the quilt more tightly around herself.

Nick reread the brief article, more slowly, taking it all in. And as he read, a steady rage built inside him. A rage that was all the more terrible for its impotence. Because the horrors the text alluded to were in the past and not to be prevented. This woman—Elizabeth—had suffered those horrors and he hadn't been there to prevent them.

A renewed surge of protectiveness eclipsed, but didn't eradicate, the fury. Tossing the paper aside, Nick didn't stop to consider his actions. He merely obeyed his instincts. Instincts that urged him up on his feet. Instincts that made him scoop Beth up and, dropping down into the chair, to cradle her on his lap, tightly clasping her against his heart.

"Darlin'," he whispered hoarsely, his lips in her hair, "that man is never gonna get near you again."

Chapter Five

Too tired to fight, Beth relaxed. How good it felt, she thought with the kind of unfocused lassitude that so often followed extreme tension, how wonderful to be held like this again. She recalled the times Grampa would cradle her on his lap and tell her stories. His voice, too, would be warm and soothing, deep and gravelly like the voice that soothed her now. And she'd feel safe, and drowsy, and content to stay like that forever—huddled against a hard, wide chest, surrounded by arms that were as gentle as they were strong and that sheltered her in a cocoon of love.

"I love you, Grampa," she murmured dreamily, snuggling closer against the warm body and more deeply into her fantasy of the past.

Only to be abruptly brought back to reality when a callused hand cupped her chin and forced her to focus on a rugged face that bore no resemblance at all to her Grampa.

"What did you say?" Nick asked tightly. He knew darned good and well what she'd said and, given the potpourri of feelings he was experiencing just then, would welcome the words—and the emotion—from the woman he held in his arms. But he hadn't heard the name she'd tagged onto the barely audible declaration, and though common sense told him it couldn't possibly have been his, he found himself half hoping it might have been.

Startled and disoriented, Beth stared into Nick's taut features, his turbulent eyes. Who...?

Cognition made her face flush scarlet. God Almighty, Dominick McCullough! She was snuggled in Nick McCullough's lap as though she belonged there!

"Let me up." Mortified, Beth struggled for release. "Nick, please..."

"Whoa, there. Settle down now." Nick wouldn't let go of her. "You and me have some talking to do."

"No..." Beth struggled anew. "Let go of me. You don't understand...."

"I understand plenty," Nick said. "I understand that you've got a husband—"

"*Ex*-husband, but—"

"Right. Ex-husband. A very important distinction."

Realizing that Beth wouldn't settle and be receptive to anything he said as long as he was holding her, Nick stood up, turned and deposited Beth back into the chair.

"I also understand that he's treated you so bad, he wound up in jail, and that now he's back on the street. That's what I understand. Now, what I'm having *trouble* understanding, is why that scares you so much, you went into hiding—

"No, let me finish now." Nick held up his hand when Beth opened her mouth to interrupt. "You changed your name and went into hiding, Elizabeth, and don't try to tell me different. What're you scared of? That he'll come after you? Find you? What are you so afraid he's going to do?"

Shivers of nerves were shaking Beth again. She wrapped her arms around herself and brought her knees up to her chest. Her lips compressed and she looked away from the harsh concern on Nick's face. He wanted to help, bless him. But what could he possibly do? How could he possibly help her, shield her? And, much more importantly, help and shield Jason?

"You don't know what he's like," she whispered, her eyes irresistibly drawn to Jason's picture on her bedside table. "You don't know what he's capable of...."

"So tell me." Nick hunkered down in front of her again. He took her hand and ignored her halfhearted attempt to pull away. "Talk to me, Elizabeth. Even if I can't do more than listen, it'll do you good to spit it out. You helped me last night," he reminded her. "The least I can do—"

"All right." She jerked her hand out of his and tossed aside the quilt. "But first let me up. I've got to move or I'll scream."

Without a word, Nick rose and moved out of the way as Beth surged off the chair and began to restlessly pace. She was frowning darkly now, and wringing her hands as she struggled to put into words the events she'd vowed never to discuss with a living soul.

To give her space, Nick shucked his hat and coat and went to sit on the edge of the bed. After watching Beth awhile, willing to wait until she was ready so speak, he idly looked at the collection of photographs that decorated the walls and the table near her bed. Family. Two older couples, parents or grandparents maybe. Another couple, young, with a little girl. The woman bore a striking resemblance to Beth. Her sister? Cousin?

And then there were pictures of a boy, again and again. From babyhood on up, always the same little boy, culminating with the eight-by-ten here on her nightstand. A handsome boy, seven or eight maybe. The dark head of curls and what-the-hell smile were the same as that guy's in the paper. That J. C. Christofferson's, the ex-husband.

And then Nick knew where he'd heard the name Christofferson before. In the post office. The day Beth had sent the parcel. Mariah had said something about Elizabeth's Jason Christofferson not being disappointed.

Jason Christofferson.

Nick looked at the picture more closely. Beth's hazel eyes minus the sadness. Her lips, full and sweetly curved. And, no, the smile was not the father's after all, it was Elizabeth's.

Jason Christofferson. Elizabeth's child.

Nick's heart began to expand and pound with excitement as he picked up the photograph and studied the boy's face. The plan that had been germinating in the back of his mind ever since he'd seen Beth's distress and read that newspaper article, now blossomed into full-blown intent.

He would cherish the mother and keep her safe. And her boy... Nick smoothed a finger across the glass in front of the photo and let a small smile soften his features. Ah, yes. Her boy. Nick swore to himself that, given the chance, he would love that little boy as if he were his own.

Across the room, Beth had stopped pacing and stood watching Nick touch the picture. The expression on the rugged man's face—an awkward sort of tenderness and longing—touched her and squeezed at her heart. She thought that here was a man who truly deserved to be a father, yet fatherhood had been denied him. Yet how many J. C. Christoffersons were out there in the world who daily abused and neglected the children with whom they'd been entrusted?

"That's Jason," she said softly. "That's my son."

"I know." With a crooked little smile, Nick nodded as he carefully replaced the frame on the nightstand. "He's got your eyes."

Beth nodded, compressing her lips against a tremor. She walked to the window and looked out on Main Street.

"He's only eight years old," she said after a silence that had been punctuated by the sound of doors slamming somewhere in the house, and hurried steps in the downstairs hall. A truck started up outside and, gears protesting, roared off out of town. "Eight years old and already he's known a lifetime of heartache. I promised him—"

She stopped to swallow. It was so darn hard for her to talk about all this. "I promised him he'd never have to cry again. That his father would never hurt either one of us again."

She dragged in another breath and bowed her head. Nick had to strain to hear what she said. "I'm so afraid that I won't be able to keep that promise."

For a moment Nick thought she was going to cry. He was half off the bed to go to her. Words rushed to his tongue, words of promise, of intent. Words that would solve Beth's problems, but that could, conceivably, complicate his life in untold measure. Words that it was prudent to leave unsaid until he'd had a chance to really think—and to sleep—on them.

And so it was with some relief that he saw Beth resolutely tilt her head and, with a deep breath and a squaring of the shoulders, regain control of herself.

"No," she said, looking up at the ceiling. "No. Don't listen to that. That was the old Beth talking, the one who was cowed and beaten, the one who was petrified of staying and just as scared of leaving for ten long, miserable years."

She spun to face him. "Dammit, I won't let him do this to Jason and me again. This time, by God, *I* will be the victor."

Her burning eyes searched his face. "You said you wanted to help. Did you mean it?"

Nick slowly approached her. "I don't generally say things I don't mean, Elizabeth."

"Good." She stared into his eyes, looking for reassurance there as she struggled to swallow her pride.

"I, uh—" She bit her lip. This was so difficult. She feared she couldn't say it, couldn't ask it. But then she had an idea.

"Wait," she blurted and rushed to the music box.

She lifted the lid and the tinkling strains of "The Minute Waltz" filled the silence as she took an old-fashioned cameo out of the box. The tune continued to play as, looking at the brooch with loving regret, she returned to Nick and offered the trinket to him.

"Here," she said. "Take it. It was my mother's—an heirloom. It's quite valuable."

At a loss, Nick took the delicate brooch. It looked incongruous in his large, work-roughened palm. "I can see that it is," he said. "It's beautiful."

He made to hand it back to Beth, but she shook her head. "I want you to keep it. As... as a form of collateral until I can pay you back."

"Pay me back?" Bemused, Nick frowned down at the cameo and then again at Beth. She was wringing her hands in an agony of embarrassment. Which only served to confuse Nick more. "Pay me back for what?"

Beth averted her eyes. "I need two thousand dollars." Her voice was so rough and low, it was almost inaudible. She looked back up at him pleadingly. "You said you wanted to help."

"And I do, but—" Nick helplessly spread his hands.

Beth went to stand by the window again, presenting him with the proud set of her shoulders. Looking beyond her, Nick saw that it had begun to snow.

"I need to get Jason and go to Canada before J.C. finds us," Beth said.

"Canada?" She might as well have said Outer Mongolia, Nick was so shaken.

"Yes." Beth half turned toward him. In the rapidly fading light, she was pale as a ghost. "It's what I've been planning all along. I've been saving nearly every penny I made at Nedda's, plus I had a few hundred dollars left from... well, from before. But it isn't enough."

She touched his arm. "Nick, I know it's a lot to ask. You hardly know me—"

"That isn't the issue, Elizabeth."

"Then you'll do it? You'll loan me the money?"

Nick broodingly studied her eager face, then frowned down again at the brooch. "What's in Canada?" he asked at length.

"Safety." In her eagerness, Beth gripped Nick's arm with both hands. Nick absently noted that it was one of the few times she'd voluntarily reached out to him. "J.C. is a felon. He can't follow us across the border. Nick—"

He looked at her face, so fervently alive with purpose and all he could think was, She wants to go away.

"I've got it all figured out," she was saying. "My mother was Canadian. Because of her, I've got dual citizenship. With what I've saved and your two thousand, Jason and I have enough of a grubstake to start—"

"I don't want you to go to Canada, Elizabeth."

"You don't—" Beth gaped at him, shocked into speechlessness.

"Beth." Nick cupped her shoulders, his voice intense. "You're an American. Your boy is an American. He ought to be raised in his own country, not among a bunch of foreigners."

"Foreigners?" Beth had found her voice. "For heaven's sake, we're talking Canada here. They speak our language. And I've even got relatives there. Family..."

"Your son is your family, Elizabeth. And he belongs here, with his own kind."

"But that's not possible!" Beth all but shouted. "Can't you see that? There is no place for us here...."

"Yes, there is." Nick took her hand and put the cameo into it. He curled her fingers around it, then went to put on his coat and hat. "I've got some thinking to do. And some checking. After which I want us to have another talk. I want you to come out to the ranch tomorrow night. I'll pick you up or you can come with Nedda, whichever suits you best. I'm giving a little party—"

"A party?" Beth stared at him as if he'd lost his mind. "With all that's transpired, you expect me to come to some ridiculous party...?"

"Yes, I do."

"Well, I'm not going to."

"Yes, you are," Nick said firmly. Then, seeing flags of indignation hoisting in her eyes, he added, "Please," with a crooked little smile. "It's just a dinner kind o' thing. Friends and relatives, all of 'em comfortable folk to be around."

"But—"

"They'll be gone by nine or so, and then you and I can talk about your problem some more. I think I might have a solution."

"But—"

"Hush," he said quietly. "Leave it be for tonight. Get some rest. I promise, if you don't like the idea I've got cooking, I'll give you the two thousand with no further argument."

He held out his hand. "Deal?"

After some hesitation, Beth took it. "Deal."

"Good." Quickly he bent and pressed his lips to her forehead, then strode to the door. "I'll have one of Nedda's girls drop your coat and handbag by here later. All right?"

Beth slowly nodded. "All right."

Nick touched the brim of his hat. "G'night, Elizabeth."

Staring at the closed door, her thoughts awhirl, Beth quietly murmured a bemused, "Good night, Nick."

Beth thought she'd never spent a longer, more miserable night. After Donna had dropped off the purse and jacket, Beth had gone down the hall to shower, for the first time wishing for something out of her former life. A Jacuzzi would have been heaven. Or even just a bathtub. There probably was one on the floor below, and she'd just as probably be more than welcome to use it. But asking Myrna would have been more trouble than Beth had deemed herself able to cope with just then. She had made do with a hot shower and crawled into bed.

Outside, the usual town noises were strangely muted all night long. The snow was falling fast and furiously, covering everything beneath a blanket of shimmering white and muffling all sound. With seventeen days to go until the holidays, Beth was sure the children of Starville thrilled at the prospect of a white Christmas.

Certainly Jason had always been especially delighted with the first few snows of winter. She and the boy would head to the knoll then for some serious sledding. Bundled up in snowsuits, they would drag the toboggan to the far end of the five-acre grounds that surrounded the mansion J.C. had bought once he'd hit the big time.

Spreading their arms, they'd let themselves fall flat on their backs and make snow angels. They'd build a snowman and, shrieking with laughter, toss snowballs at each other.

Sometimes J.C. would come out and throw snowballs, too. Only he'd pack the snow tightly and throw to hurt. He'd aim for spots that were vulnerable, hurting Beth, hurting Jason, and making Jason cry.

Which would infuriate J.C. Cursing, he'd stomp back into the house and leave them, their fun spoiled.

Not that last time, though. Just about two years ago now. That time he'd grabbed the boy, had shaken him and yelled at him to stop sniveling.

"Stop it!" Beth had thrown herself bodily between them. "J.C., you're hurting him!"

Snarling, J.C. had turned on Beth. Hauling back his arm, he'd slapped her face. "Butt out when I'm dealing with my son!"

"But you're hurting him!"

"I'm teaching him to be a man!"

"Mommy! Mommy!" Jason had gone for his dad like a little tiger, pummeling the large man with his little mittened fists. "Leave her alone. I hate you! I hate you!"

"See what you've done?" *Wham,* another slap.

Beth's ears were ringing. Blood gushed from her nose. Her knees threatened to buckle. She gritted her teeth. Locked her knees.

"You've turned the boy against me. I'll get you for that."

Reaching down, the big man brushed Jason off his leg, flinging him into the snow like some pesky bug, before, with a last vicious curse, he did the same to Beth.

She lay there, eyes closed, panting. Vowing, never again. This was it. This was the last time.

Jason crawled over to her. He laid his cold, tear-stained cheek against Beth's. She stirred then. Rolled over and fiercely clutched the boy to her. Together, they wept.

That afternoon, while J.C. was at practice, Beth had packed up a few of their belongings and escaped. She had gone with Jason to a women's shelter, and from there had called an attorney.

"Are we safe now, Mommy?" Jason had asked.

And Beth had said, "Yes, darling. We're safe."

Except, they hadn't been. After the divorce, J.C. had found them.

And now, yet another year later, tossing and turning on her bed in Starville, Beth knew he would find them again.

It was all Beth could do to get through the day. If she'd bothered to give the matter some thought, she might have figured the snow would keep people home, slow down business. But she would have figured wrong. It seemed the ranchers and farmers, as well as the townfolk, took the snow in their stride. Their vehicles, if not four-wheel drive, were outfitted with whatever traction devices were deemed appropriate and off, it seemed, they went.

Certainly there was no slack time at Nedda's, for which Beth gave thanks. She needed to stay busy in order to keep herself from going crazy. She dreaded the dinner party, told Nedda she wouldn't go, only to change her mind and tell her she would. Nedda took Beth's behavior with unruffled calm. She asked no questions and made no comments.

Whatever Nick might or might not have told her and the other waitresses, as the day progressed, it became clear to Beth that nobody seemed inclined to pry or intrude.

She loved them for this with a surge of emotion so fierce, the thought of packing up and leaving for Canada in the next few days brought an ache to her heart that was ten times as strong as the pain she'd felt at leaving her home in Chicago.

These were wonderful, decent people here in Starville. These were people who, in quiet, unobtrusive ways, showed they cared.

Nick McCullough was one of those people. Sure, he'd come on a bit forceful last night, deciding Beth would attend his party whether she wanted to or not. Deciding he knew what was best for her. Taking charge. Taking over.

But nicely. Not threateningly. Not in a way that made Beth feel as if she weren't in charge of her life. Not the way J.C. had always ridden roughshod, beating her down when she'd dared to protest.

Nick McCullough...

Staring into her coffee, forgetting Charley who was going on about something or other across from her in the backmost booth, Beth savored the warm glow that spread through her at the thought of Nick's name. What a man he was. For all his brawn, so gentle. For all his severity, so sensitive at times. For all his rugged manly pride, not above sharing his pain and making himself vulnerable.

What a friend he was.

The realization startled Beth. Nick McCullough, her friend. Somehow, though she'd promised herself not to make any, she had made a friend of one of the wealthiest ranchers around.

And, looking across the table at the happily chatting cook, she knew she'd made another one in Charley Rider, as well as—Beth exchanged a smile with the boss lady at the cash register—in Nedda Lewis.

A sharp ache pierced Beth's heart. She hadn't wanted to make friends for the very reasons that were now making her hurt. She had to leave, leave this place and these people who had become so dear to her in spite of herself. Unless—

Nick wanted to speak with her. He hadn't liked the idea of her leaving the country. He'd said he had some thinking to do. Some checking to do.

Thinking about what? Checking into what? What was he up to? Could there possibly be some way...?

Beth quickly slammed the door on that hopeful train of thought. There was no way. Period. She had to leave. J.C. was relentless, his threats were not idle. If she had learned nothing else in her ten years with him, it was this. He always meant what he said.

He would find her. If she stayed in this country, maiden name or not, he *would* find her.

And he would find Jason.

Kathy Grimes wasn't anyone J.C. knew well—she was a childhood friend and college roommate of Beth's who'd buried herself in the mountains of Vermont years ago. But he did know of her, and he would hire detectives. Eventually, all too soon, Jason's whereabouts would become known to J.C.

Gathering up the remnants of her mostly uneaten lunch, Beth slid out of the booth. She resolved to go to Nick's dinner party and to listen to what he had to say. But afterward she would ask him for the money. And then she would leave Starville, send for Jason, and head across the border for Whitehorse in the Yukon Territory.

Beth didn't agonize over what to wear to the Triple Creek Ranch. She'd gone to many dinner parties in her life with J.C.; it had been part of the image. Some had been formal, others not. All had been elegant. Often the press had been there and, as the wife of a hockey superstar, she'd been required to dress to dazzle the media, the fans, the owners.

Beth didn't dress to dazzle tonight. Given the weather, the locale and the people, she chose a simple black wool, completely unaware that in its very simplicity the frock would set her apart.

She applied a minimum of makeup and swept her hair back from her face with a comb behind each ear. As her only jewelry, she wore the half-carat diamond studs that had been her wedding gift from her grandmother.

She was waiting at the front step when Nedda's husband, Frank, pulled his Chevy Blazer to a skidding stop outside the rooming house door.

"Lordy, girl, don't you have sense enough to wear boots in weather like this?" Nedda exclaimed with a disapproving glance at Beth's slim black pumps. "What if we get stuck?"

"Ain't plannin' to, Ned," Frank told his wife. "So leave the girl alone."

Settling into the back seat, Beth smiled to herself. It had been a long time since anyone had called her a girl and even longer since she'd felt like one. Even though, at thirty-three, she might not be old by most standards, she'd felt for a long time like the weight of the world rested on her shoulders. Carefree girlhood seemed aeons in the past.

Driving out of town, all the houses and buildings wearing their new, white top hats of snow, Beth noted that people had put their Christmas lights up. Here and there a lighted Christmas tree could be spied, too, and the radio was playing some merry preholiday tune.

Christmas was fast approaching. Beth should have felt sad. At the best of times, she tended to get nostalgic at this time of year. But this evening, strangely, she didn't. Instead, what she was feeling was a tingling sense of anticipation. A sense of good things to come.

It was probably the knowledge that she'd be together with Jason for the holiday after all this year, even if in some place as far away as the Canadian North.

"I can't believe it's almost Christmas," Nedda groused from the front seat. "I haven't done a lick o' shopping. How 'bout you?" she asked Beth.

"I sent a parcel last week," Beth said. "And that's all the presents I need to worry about."

"Not planning to get Nick anything?"

"Well, I—" Beth hadn't even considered that a gift for Nick might be appropriate. And, of course, it wouldn't be, even if—in the event Nick wouldn't lend her the money—she should find herself still in Starville for the holiday. "Actually, no."

"Hmm" was all Nedda said to that, leaving Beth with the vague impression that she'd somehow disappointed the woman.

"What are you two doing for Christmas this year?" she asked to bridge the—to her—awkward pause.

"We gen'rally go to our daughter's in Walla Walla," Frank replied. "'Spect we'll do it this year, too. Won't we, Ned?"

"Hmm," Nedda said again.

"Always like to see the grandkids at Christmas," said Frank. "Daughter's got a boy, three, and a—"

"We been driving past Triple Creek land for the past ten minutes now," Nedda interrupted Frank's proud recital. "And the land goes on for miles in the other direction, too. Pretty well fixed, is Nick McCullough. You know that, don't you, Beth?"

"Well, I sort of gathered as much from what—"

"A girl could do a lot worse than Nick McCullough," Nedda said, sending Beth a stern, meaningful look. "He's loosened up since you come to town. Looks a lot happier, too."

Ill at ease with the drift of Nedda's talk, Beth said nothing to that.

"Hasn't had a party since that Susan got killed. And we sure's shootin' didn't get invited while she was alive, I can tell you. She was a snooty sort."

Another meaningful glance was sent toward Beth. "Nick tell you about Susan?"

Beth bit down on her lower lip to keep a smile from forming. It had just occurred to her, the way Nedda was going on... Why, the old she-devil was matchmaking! "Um, yes. As a matter of fact, he did."

"It wasn't his fault, you know."

"Uh-huh."

"Never could understand what he saw in her."

"Nedda . . ." Frank's tone held a warning.

"Well, it's true. She was so darn stuck-up all the time. And treatin' him like—"

"Woman, that's enough," Frank said sternly. To Beth's surprise, Nedda didn't argue, only stuck out her lower lip and stared out of her window while Frank gave Beth a look of apology in the rearview mirror.

"That's the Triple Creek gate comin' up," Nedda said after a minute. Beth leaned forward to see the Blazer's headlights illuminate three massive, stripped logs forming a portal across the side road into which they were turning.

"This is Nick's driveway now," Nedda continued in her role as tour guide-cum-yenta. "We're on Triple Creek land. That's pasture and fallow fields on both sides of us."

"I see." Actually, Beth saw very little through the curtain of densely falling snow.

"The drive's about a mile long."

"Really." That was impressive, all right. Beth strained for a glimpse of the ranch house Nedda was saying lay just beyond that stand of evergreens and naked poplars.

And then there it was. Splendid, sprawling, built entirely of thick, stripped logs that had been weathered as attractively by age and exposure as had Nick McCullough's facial features. The house was ablaze with lights beyond the deep porch that spanned it.

Frank pulled right up to the porch steps so that, as he gallantly put it, his ladies wouldn't have to get their feet cold and wet, then went to park his truck amidst the many similar vehicles that already crowded the roomy yard.

Beyond the parked cars and pickups, Beth could vaguely distinguish more trees and some large outbuildings bordering the yard, but with Nedda urging her along to the massive, carved ranch house door, she didn't get a chance to really look around.

Music and a babble of voices could be heard from inside the house. Through the wall-size window on the left, Beth could see a crowd of people mingling and chatting. Knowing that to knock would be futile, Nedda just opened the door and, with Beth in tow, stepped into the welcoming warmth of the house.

They were in a vestibule from which the room with most of the guests could be entered through an open archway. Undoing her coat while Nedda struggled out of rubber overshoes, Beth discreetly perused the people in the other room. Some looked familiar, patrons of the diner. None seemed aware of her and Nedda's arrival.

But then she saw a tall, ruggedly handsome man in an elegant Western-cut suit separate himself from a cluster of men and briskly stride toward them.

Nick. Beth's eyes widened at the sight of him. His eyes, alight with something that sent a delicious tremor through her limbs, were locked on hers from beneath fine, dark eyebrows. His hair, not mussed and flattened from his hat for once, was combed back from his face in a way that most attractively accentuated the manly planes and valleys of his weathered features. The suit hugged his tall, rangy frame like a loving embrace, bringing out the width of his shoulders, the breadth of his powerful chest, the steel-hewn length and leanness of loin and legs.

Watching him make his way toward her, and for the first time noting the loose-limbed grace of him, Beth's mouth went dry.

"Hello, Elizabeth." He was in front of her, taking both of her hands in his and greeting her in a tone so warm and mellow, Beth had to swallow to relieve the constriction her unnerved reaction had put in her throat. She moistened her lips and felt her face flush as Nick's gaze shifted to the lick of her tongue.

Thoroughly rattled, she barely managed a choked "Hello," and was ever so glad when Nedda, overshoes and coat in hand, interrupted.

"Where are you puttin' people's wraps, Nick?"

"Two doors down." Nick glanced at Nedda, but didn't release Beth's hands. "In the master bedroom."

Nedda shuffled off and Nick's gaze returned to Beth's. She had used the interval to gain control over her wayward response to him, though her heartbeat was still far from normal.

"I should go with her," she said, hoping he wouldn't notice the breathlessness in her voice. "I've still got my coat on."

Nick's gaze shifted. "So you do. Here—" he released her hands and slid the full-length cashmere off Beth's shoulders "—let me show you where it goes."

He'd captured her hand again and was tugging her along. Nedda, fluffing her hair, was coming toward them. Seeing them hand in hand, she beamed.

"There's drinks in the living room," Nick told her. "Cyrus is playing bartender. Cy's my ranch foreman," he explained to Beth who had trouble thinking beyond the fact that the feel of her hand in his much bigger one was playing havoc with her senses.

"And here's where the coats are," Nick said, adding hers to the mound of outerwear already heaped on the massive king-size bed. She looked around the room. Solid mahogany and an absence of frills.

He pointed to a door at the opposite end of the room. "Bathroom's through there, if you need to freshen up."

"No, I'm fine."

Nick's lingering gaze told her he agreed, and Beth's cheeks flushed.

"There's another bath by the other bedroom," he said, tucking her hand up against his chest, forcing Beth to stand close in front of him and tilt back her head to meet his compelling gaze. "This is an old house," he murmured, "built before the advent of powder rooms and other such amenities. Later, I'll give you a tour, if you like."

Beth, swallowing, merely nodded. Nick's gaze swept her face and fastened on her mouth. "I'm glad you came, Elizabeth."

She watched him say it, watched his finely etched lips as he spoke, felt his breath on her face as he brought his own closer.

"Really glad," he said, just as their mouths touched. The kiss, if that was what this feather-light touching could be called, was over before Beth could react. His lips now brushed the knuckles of her still-imprisoned hand. His eyes, still locked on hers, glowed. But though their heat sent further shivers through Beth's already quivering senses, she felt no threat, no disquiet, no apprehension about Nick's intent. She knew instinctively that here was a man who'd never pressure, never push beyond whatever boundaries a woman chose to establish.

"Come on," he said, tucking her hand into the crook of his arm. "Let me introduce you around."

The last of the guests were gone. Nick came back in the house and, with a sigh of relief, closed the front door. The party had gone well. Everybody, himself included, had had a good time. His family and friends had taken to Elizabeth just as he'd known they would. And she had seemed to like them, too.

He walked back into the living room. Jeanie and Cy were cleaning up. Beth had gone to freshen up.

"Great spread, Jean," Nick told her. And clapping Cyrus on the back, he added with a chuckle, "You're one hell of a bartender, bud."

He picked up some glasses and followed the Mulligans into the kitchen. "Let's leave the rest o' this till morning." He set his load on the counter. "Is there any coffee left?"

"In that white carafe over there." Jean closed the dishwasher door and turned on the machine. "There's some dessert left in the icebox, should you want some."

"Thanks." Nick closed the back door behind the couple who'd been on the ranch since he was in his teens. He didn't know how he could have managed without them all these years and hoped he wouldn't have to for a good many more. Right now, however, he only wanted them gone so that he and Elizabeth could finally be alone.

He watched them trudge through the snow to their own house, some hundred yards across the backyard, then turned just as Beth stepped into the kitchen.

In her sleek dress and simple hairstyle, she was a vision of understated elegance. Her quiet dignity had endeared her to his guests this evening; she had talked with them easily and, on their part, there'd been none of the wary reserve with which they usually treated folks from the city. They had accepted Beth as just another guest at Nick McCullough's party.

But would they accept her as Nick McCullough's wife?

Chapter Six

Getting a mite ahead o' yourself, aren't you, friend?

Yeah, Nick thought with an inward, self-mocking smile. *You* might think marrying her is a good idea, but...

"How about some coffee?" he asked, seeking to hide his sudden attack of the jitters behind the role of thoughtful host. He crossed to where the carafe sat on the counter. "Jean says there's dessert left, too. If you'd care for some...?"

"No, nothing more for me, thanks. It's all been so delicious."

Beth's smile seemed a little uncertain around the edges. It told Nick that she was nervous, too. It made him feel better, more in charge.

"I'll just pour myself some then," he said, taking a mug out of the cupboard and filling it. "And then we can go into my study."

"Nick..." Beth put a hand to her constricting throat. She tried to clear the roughness from her voice, telling herself she was silly to be ill at ease about being alone with Nick in the house. There was nothing between them but a friendship of sorts....

Except that he'd kissed her by the coats in the bedroom. And that all night long she'd caught him looking at her with... well, with a *gleam* in his eye. A masculine gleam that made her very aware of her femininity and that caused her pulse to flutter. It fluttered even now, just being in the same room again and thinking about those glances.

"Nick," she said again. "I, uh, I know we sort of agreed to talk some more after the party...." Deep breath. "But I'm really rather tired. I think I should've gone home with Nedda after all. I—"

"Elizabeth." A steaming mug of coffee in one hand, Nick gripped her elbow with the other and steered her out of the kitchen and into his study across the hall. "Relax."

He pressed her into one of the two leather armchairs fronting his desk, then set down his coffee and went to a cabinet that was part of a glassed-in bookcase. He took out a bottle of brandy and two snifters. Back at his desk, he splashed a finger of the amber liquid into each glass and handed one to Beth.

She didn't really want any, but took the glass to have something around which to wrap her nervous hands.

Nick took a seat behind the desk, shuffled some papers out of the way and positioned his brandy and coffee. He was giving himself, and Beth, a moment to settle down, just as their seating arrangement was intended to reinforce the illusion that the forthcoming talk would be strictly business.

The stage set, Nick took a breath and opened his mouth to speak. But he immediately closed it again as he realized he had not a clue how to start. He lifted his brandy glass. Noting that his hand was suddenly no longer steady, he took a healthy swallow to brace himself. The liquor was a smooth flame slithering down his throat and into his stomach, creating a pool of reassuring warmth.

"Elizabeth." His voice sounded almost normal, Nick was glad to find. "I, uh, I want you to think carefully about what I'm going to propose to you. Before you give me an answer, I mean."

He was botching this, he could tell by Beth's gathering frown.

Nick took another bracing swig of brandy before, keeping his eyes on the glass, he carefully set it down. "I've been giving this a lot of thought and, frankly, I've come to the conclusion that the best solution to your, uh, problem would be to, uh, to marry me."

There, he'd said it. He risked a cautious glance at Beth from beneath lowered brows.

Her expression and incredulous "What!" made him wince. Rubbing his forehead, he offered a wry, twisted smile.

"Now you know why I'd never make it as a diplomat," he said. "I tend to barge in where angels fear to tread, or however that saying goes."

Beth said nothing, only continued to stare at him as if he'd sprouted horns.

Sighing, Nick dropped his hand and settled back in his chair with assumed calm and casualness. "Let me try and do better. Just listen a minute," he added when Beth began steadily shaking her head.

"If you'll only think about it, it'll make sense. You and that boy of yours've been through hell. It's in your eyes for all to see, Elizabeth, the pain of it. How hard it's been. And it must've been even harder on...Jason, is it?"

Compressing her lips, Beth nodded.

"He's just a little boy," Nick continued persuasively. "Just a little feller who's lost everything—his home, his friends, his mother and dad. And now you want him to lose his country, too? Elizabeth..."

Nick rounded the desk and planted himself in front of Beth. She wouldn't look at him, only stared into the brandy she was clutching so hard with both hands, her knuckles were white.

"Elizabeth, I could give Jason a home here. And you. Both of you. You'd be safe on the ranch. The town is small, strangers are noticed. We—you—would hear about it right away if anyone came around asking questions. And people around here sure's hell wouldn't give a stranger much more than the time o' day.

"But likely as not, it wouldn't even come to that. You'd have my name to give you anonymity. You'd be Elizabeth McCullough, and we could have Jason be called McCullough, too. That ex-husband of yours would have no way—"

"You underestimate him."

Beth's quiet interjection encouraged Nick to press on. "Maybe I do and maybe I don't. Could be you *over*estimate the man's determination and—"

"No." Beth raised her eyes at last. They were wide and filled with an agonized kind of bleakness. "You don't know that he's like, what he's capable of..."

Beth hesitated, then lifted the snifter to her lips and tossed back the entire contents. She gasped, coughed and shook herself. Bowing her head, she sucked in a long and shaky breath.

"He hates me," she said in a choked little voice. "After the divorce, he broke into the house a friend of mine let me use while she and her husband were in Europe. It was the middle of the night. Jason and I were asleep. J.C. wasn't supposed to know where we were, but somehow..."

She shook her head as if to banish the haunting visions. "He'd hired a detective. And he, uh, he found us. He broke into the house. Smashed the window next to the front door and simply let himself in. By the time the alarm was activated—"

"Elizabeth." Nick couldn't stand to see the pain it was causing Beth to tell him all this. There was no doubt in his mind that her ex was a prime piece of work. She didn't have to try and convince him.

But Beth brushed aside Nick's concern with an angry shake of the head. "Listen to this, Nick," she said harshly. "And believe what I'm saying. If I stay in this country, he *will* find us, just like he found us before. That time he managed to only break three of my ribs and give me two black eyes and a concussion before the police arrived and took him away. But the next time he'll kill me. He swore he would."

"Not as long as there's breath in my body." Leaning forward, Nick clasped Beth's shoulders and gave her a little shake. "Marry me, Elizabeth. Let me keep you safe. Both of you."

Beth stared at him. She heard the fervor of his tone, saw the honest zeal in the depths of his sky-blue eyes and was touched by the intensity of purpose and compassion that was stamped in every line of his face. More than anything she wanted to believe him.

Her eyes dropped to his lips. She remembered their fleeting touch with a renewed quickening of her senses. She felt the warmth of his hands on her shoulders, felt the heat of his body enveloping her like a cozy blanket. The breadth of his chest and shoulders looming over her hinted of muscles that were hard and sleek from honest labor, inviting the exploration of her hands. Their bulk blocked out the rest of the room, making her feel dainty and feminine and isolated from peril. Safe.

He was strong. All man and undeniably sexy. He was everything a woman could possibly wish for in a man. If a man—and marriage—were what the woman wanted.

But it wasn't. Not for this woman. This woman could not afford to relinquish even a small part of herself to a man ever again. This woman dare not marry again. Not now. Not ever. Not even a man such as Nick McCullough.

Reaching up, she touched Nick's cheek. Nick thought he saw regret in her eyes, but maybe that was just wishful thinking because she said, "Thank you," softly, but with unmistakable implacability.

"You're a good man," she said. "And I appreciate what you're trying to do, but don't you see? For me, marriage is out of the question."

"It doesn't have to be." Nick didn't budge. Her palm against his cheek warmed him. He mourned the loss of that warmth when she took the hand away. "It could work for us. I'm not like him, Elizabeth."

"God, I know that." Beth closed her eyes, only to open them again, beseechingly. "But I don't love you, Nick. And, given my history, I doubt I ever could."

That hurt, though Nick knew it made no sense that it should. "This isn't about love," he said gruffly. "Love has nothing to do with this."

"Then what has? Why do you want this?"

Those were good questions, but Nick didn't like them. Wasn't ready for them. They forced him to come up with a sufficiently convincing motive, something he hadn't been able to do as he'd plotted this course.

Abruptly he straightened and walked around to the other side of his desk. He picked up the snifter and drained it. Deep in thought, he took the bottle and poured himself some more. What could he tell her that would make sense? That would satisfy her, make her feel as though this was merely tit for tat. I wash your hands, you wash mine. That kind o' thing.

Absently, he gestured with the bottle toward Beth and, when she signaled her refusal with a quick shake of the head, plunked it down on the desk and pushed in the stopper.

And all the while his mind was trying furiously to come up with a plausible reason for his wanting to marry Elizabeth. A plausible reason other than the one he suspected to be true but wasn't about to confess to her at this time.

He had fallen in love with Elizabeth Coleman.

Damn it all anyway!

With a not-quite-steady hand, Nick took the glass and would have drained it if he hadn't caught Beth's unmistakable alarm.

"What?" He set the glass down so hard, some of the liquor splashed onto the desk. "*He* used to drink—is that it?"

"Yes."

"And then he'd get nasty."

"Nasty-*er,*" Beth said. "Toward the end, he was always nasty. Drinking just made it worse."

"I'm not a drinker, Elizabeth."

"I know that. But you seemed so angry—"

"How?"

"How what?"

"How do you know I'm not a drinker?"

Discomfited and bemused by Nick's sudden and somber intensity, Beth shrugged a little uncertainly. "Why, I. . . I guess I sense it."

"And do you also sense that I'd never hurt you?"

"I— Yes."

He was around the desk and back in front of her. He took the empty glass she was still clutching and, setting it aside, caught both of her hands in his.

"Then marry me, Elizabeth."

"No."

Nick ignored that. "You'd be helping me out as much or more than I'd be helping you," he insisted, improvising on the solution that had just that moment presented itself to him. "Jean is getting on. Hell, she's sixty-five next month and not in the best of health. Cy's sixty-eight. They've got kids who're married and living all over creation. Jeanie wants time to go visit with them, time to get to know her grandkids. But she won't take that time because she says she can't leave me here to fend for myself.

"And she's right. I'm no cook and I sure's hell am not equipped to run the ranch and clean house, too. There's some women in town I could hire, but, frankly, I'm not the easiest man to get along with. There's not a lot o' people I like."

He stopped, searching Beth's eyes for reactions and feelings. What he saw, or rather what he didn't see, namely outright rejection, encouraged him. Enough to say, very softly, "But I like you, Elizabeth. And I think you kinda like me, too."

"Oh, for heaven's sake!" Flustered, because Nick's huskily whispered words had snuck past her defenses and touched something she'd guarded—her heart—Beth jerked her hands out of his and, pushing him aside, jumped to her feet. She took a few steps to put some space between them, exclaiming, "I like Charley Rider, too, but that doesn't mean I'd be willing to marry him!"

Nick didn't say anything. He was encouraged by her reaction. She no longer flatly refused him, was obviously doing some thinking. He crossed his arms and leaned back against the desk, content to watch her pace.

"It's a ridiculous notion," she said after a while.

Nick shook his head. "It makes perfect sense. We each get what we want. I get a housekeeper, and you get—"

"Married." Beth finished with a snort. "Which I do not want to be." She stopped in front of him. Glared up at him. "Because, Mr. McCullough, in my book, marriage is equal to a life sentence."

"It wouldn't have to be."

"Really." Her brows arched into a "this had better be good" expression. "Are you saying the laws of matrimony are different in the state of Washington?"

"Ordinarily, no, but—" Nick was thinking fast and hard. "But there are ways to mitigate those laws. I was thinking of a prenuptial agreement of sorts."

"Oh?"

She sounded skeptical, but also vaguely intrigued. Nick mentally rubbed his hands and pressed on. "Yes. You've heard of term limitations for politicians? Well, I was thinking we could put a term limitation on this marriage."

"Really."

She was staring into his eyes. Definitely intrigued, Nick decided, and his heart began to pound. "We could draw up a paper stating that after a given period of time—two years, say..."

"One year would be the most I'd agree to," Beth injected.

Nick had a hard time suppressing the smile that filled his chest. "All right," he said agreeably. "Let's make it one year. We'll both sign a statement saying that after one year of marriage, if either one of us wants out, the other will agree to a divorce—"

"Annulment."

Their gazes tangled and in the profound silence that followed, meshed. Neither spoke, but all manner of potent messages were exchanged. Messages that had Beth's heart pumping fast and furiously and that filled Nick with a longing and hope so vast, it was all he could do to keep his hands at his sides instead of using them to haul Beth into his arms.

With effort he kept his voice steady and his gaze level on Beth's. "Divorce, Elizabeth."

His meaning was crystal-clear to her. A shiver, delicious but, at the same time, infinitely frightening, slithered down Beth's back. She swallowed a strangely exciting feeling of apprehension that made her throat tickle. "You mean," she started, and had to stop and swallow because her voice shook so bad. "You mean we...you... It wouldn't be a marriage in name only?"

"Elizabeth..." Nick reached for her, but Beth stepped out of reach. "Would you really want it to be?"

Beth hugged herself as another shiver shriveled her skin. Her emotions were at war with her saner self. After a while she felt strong enough to nod. "Yes," she managed in a choked little whisper. "Yes, I would."

She saw something flare in Nick's eyes—disappointment, hurt?—and quickly turned her back. Released from the mesmerizing force of his gaze, sanity returned with a rush. She laughed, an off-key, self-conscious sound.

"Listen to us," she said. "Talking as if, as if everything's settled but the details."

"As far as I'm concerned, everything *is* settled," Nick said quietly from behind her.

"Well, it's not." Beth spun to face him, shaken and angry. Angry because she'd been tempted. Was still tempted when common sense and hard-won experience told her that Nick made everything sound way too simple. Impossibly simple. "It's not and it won't be. It can't be."

"It can, if you want it."

"Well, I don't want it." Her hands fisted. Resisting Nick's too-simple offer was like swimming against an outgoing tide. It took all her strength to prevail.

"I'm sorry, Nick." Beth forced herself to relax and gentle her tone. Nick was grim-faced and pale. She felt a need to mend fences, told herself that was silly, but wanted to reach out and comfort him, just the same. But nothing about him said he'd welcome the gesture and so, miserable, she stared at his set profile until she couldn't stand it any longer and said, "Look, I really am sorry, Nick. I really do appreciate what you're trying to do for me. This isn't personal—"

"Let it go, Elizabeth." Though Nick's expression was still somber when he faced her at last, Beth thought she detected a glimmer of humor in his steady gaze. "Come here," he said.

Puzzled and a little wary, Beth nevertheless did as he asked, stopping about a foot in front of him.

He drew her closer.

Alarm bells went off in Beth's head even as her blood quickened with the feel of his body against hers. "Nick..."

"Quit worrying so much."

"But," Beth began again, only to have Nick silence her with his lips.

With none of the hesitation he had earlier displayed, his mouth claimed Beth's in scorching possession. Hungrily, he invaded her sweetness with his tongue and captured hers.

For a moment, overwhelmed, surprised, off guard and filled with a violent longing and need that matched his, Beth relaxed against him and responded. Her hands, caught between their bodies, uncurled and flattened against his chest. She felt the thunder of his heart; its galloping pace matched her own. She widened her mouth, welcomed his tongue and stroked it with her own. The pleasure of it was like nothing she'd ever experienced. His taste—coffee, brandy and desire—was headier than the finest champagne. Her blood sang as it raced, hotly, sweetly, through her veins.

His hand smoothed the length of her back, the curve of her waist, her hips, and settled on the swell of her buttocks. He urged her closer with that hand, closer against his hips, and the rigid proof of his hunger.

Feeling it, feeling herself wanting to turn liquid in response to it, Beth stiffened. Her hands pushed where seconds before, briefly, they'd itched to touch naked skin. Her protest, though muffled by Nick's kiss, was unnecessary because at the first hint of resistance, Nick had reined himself in.

Though it cost him, cost him dearly, he'd had long years in which to practice self-discipline and control.

Besides which, this was one lady he'd never in his life want to hurt or in any way coerce.

Looking into her eyes, seeing the turmoil there, the lingering traces of passion as well as confusion and a spark of indignation, he took comfort in the fact that, whatever else she might feel toward him, indifference was not part of the package.

The drive from the ranch back to Starville through what was practically a blizzard had been slow, and silent. Nick had had his hands and mind full keeping the four-by-four on the road and out of snowdrifts. Beth had been in such a state of nerves—from their discussion, she told herself though she couldn't stop tingling from Nick's unexpected kiss—as to be all but catatonic.

She had roused herself sufficiently in front of the rooming house to take note of the weather and to ask if Nick would be all right driving home. She had known only relief when he'd assured her he'd be fine. With a hurriedly mumbled "Good night," she had scrambled out of the vehicle and, without looking back, had run into the house.

Sleep had been late in coming; dreams had prevented proper rest. She'd come awake on a scream, her face wet, her limbs tangled in bed sheets that were damp from her sweat.

It was six o'clock Sunday morning. The rooming house was as quiet as a tomb. All the other tenants were, no doubt, sleeping the sleep of the just.

Dragging the quilt with her, Beth got out of bed. She wrapped the cottony warmth around herself and went to stand by the window. Outside, it was still pitch-dark but the meager and spotty pools of illumination from Main Street's three street lamps showed that the snow had stopped falling. Everything visible sparkled beneath a pristine blanket of snow. The tire tracks from Nick's truck had been eliminated.

Winter wonderland. Unbidden, the strains of that song and bits of the lyrics popped into Beth's head. "... are you listenin'? Da-da-dum, snow is glistenin'...."

Ah, Jason, you'd love it here. Beth's head fell forward and rested against the cold window glass. *Jason, what am I going to do... ?*

She turned to glance at the clock: six-thirty. That meant it was nine-thirty in Vermont....

Dropping the quilt, Beth grabbed her coat and shrugged into it. Then she picked up the jar of coins she'd collected for phone calls and hurried quietly down the stairs to where the pay phone was located in the hall one floor below.

"Kathy?" she said in a near whisper a few moments later, hunched over the phone so that no one else would hear her speak. "It's me, Beth. No, I'm fine. Except... J.C. is out, Kath..."

Listening to Kathy's exclamation of shock, followed immediately by a barrage of reassurances, Beth couldn't help but smile. Five-foot-nothing in her highest heels, Kathy Grimes was nevertheless not a woman who was easily intimidated.

"I know Jason's in good hands with you," Beth injected into the first momentary lull. "He's safer with you than with anyone else I can think of. But still, I worry, Kath. Yes, yes, I know. It doesn't accomplish anything. Is he there? Could I just talk to him a minute?"

Waiting while Kathy fetched Jason away from his Sunday breakfast pancakes, Beth closed her eyes and drew a shaky breath. She was thinking, *she* should be the one making him pancakes. And that *she* should be the one keeping him safe.

"Yes, love, Mommy's here," she said, her eyes popping open when Jason spoke her name with a glad catch in his high-pitched voice. "Lucky you, eating Aunt Kathy's yummy pancakes... How are you, sweetie...? I miss you, too. So much. All the time."

Beth heard him start to cry and her own throat closed. Her vision blurred as he asked when she was going to come for him. When would he see her?

"Soon," she promised fiercely, vowing that one way or the other, it really would be. "Very, very soon." When her tears were making it impossible to speak without betraying her emotional upset to Jason who needed her to be strong, she added, "Look, I have to hang up now but I'll call you again a little later, okay? I love you, sweetie...."

With a hand that shook, Beth fumbled to replace the receiver, then pressed her forehead against the wall's cool plasterboard for a moment in an effort to compose herself. She held her breath to suppress the sob rising painfully into her throat, then slowly turned and made her way up the stairs to her room.

Once there, she was at a loss as to what to do next. Her brief talk with Jason had drained her, but had not brought her any closer to reaching a decision.

After a while, knowing she wouldn't stop worrying and fretting with nothing but an idle Sunday morning on her hands, Beth went and took a shower. Afterward, she heated a kettle for a cup of instant coffee, ate a banana, then stripped the bed and put on clean sheets. When it was eight o'clock and she deemed it all right to possibly disturb the other residents, she gathered up the rest of her dirty laundry and went down to the basement laundry room.

As her washing was agitated, rinsed and then tumbling in the dryer, Beth paced and agonized. Her head hurt from all the thinking and fretting she'd done. She tried to be rational and objective in her reasoning. She tried to weigh the pros and the cons of Nick's proposal.

For instance, would taking Jason to Canada really be such a good idea? Kindred spirits or not, Canadians *were* foreigners in that they were *not* American. This had never struck Beth as a big deal before—she was half-Canadian herself, after all, and her mother had never seemed to her different from anybody else's mom.

Also, in hockey, quite a few of J.C.'s teammates had been Canadian and the only difference between them and their American counterparts had been that some of them spoke French as their first language.

Before Nick had brought up the importance of raising Jason among his own kind rather than abroad, Beth had never thought of Canada as being *abroad.* To her, the border separating it from the U.S. had seemed more of a symbolic rather than *real* barrier.

So, would she be depriving Jason of his birthright by taking him out of the country? Would she be denying him something of vital importance, namely his roots?

No.

Beth shook out a towel and, her motions jerky with agitation, briskly folded it in thirds. No, dammit.

She was letting Nick McCullough's arguments get to her. And—she hated to admit it, but it was shamefully true—she was letting the remembered feel of Nick's mouth on hers, of his hands on her body, intrude and even overshadow her many other, more sane and reasonable considerations.

She was carrying her neat stack of clean laundry upstairs when something occurred to her that froze her steps.

J.C. had made many good friends in Canada in the course of his illustrious hockey career. What made her think she'd be safe from him there?

The man had connections. He was devious, angry and determined. How could she think he'd let a little thing like the friendly border between two kindred nations stand between him and his goal? A goal that consisted of finding her and—

No.

Beth resolutely clamped down on a burgeoning sense of panic. Enough. She was letting hysteria do her thinking.

Her course was set, she grimly reminded herself as she climbed the rest of the way up to her room. Marriage was *not,* could not be, a viable alternative.

Beth, glad to escape the confines of her room and the turmoil of her thoughts, went to work at ten-thirty. Nedda opened up shop at eleven to cater to the after-church crowd wanting breakfast or brunch. The diner closed again at two.

Nedda seemed surprised to see her. "Didn't think Nick woulda made it into town to take you back home," she said.

"He took the four-wheel drive." Beth tried to sound offhand as she tied on the clean little square of apron they were issued daily to wear over the uniform. She and Nedda were the only ones on duty that Sunday, outside of Charley of course, who was busy firing up the kitchen.

"Didn't think you'd make it into work, neither." Nedda cast her an arch look. "Thought you mighta spent the night at the ranch."

"Now why would you think a thing like that?" Beth was proud of her steady hands, working alongside her boss. Quickly and efficiently, she arranged napkins and silverware on the place mats in the booths and on the counter. Business would start at eleven o'clock sharp; the church was just three blocks down the road.

"'Cause I seen the way Nick McCullough looks at you, is why. That man is smitten."

Smitten. Beth felt her ears grow hot. She remembered those looks of Nick's only too well, and if the way thoughts of that man's kisses kept creeping unbidden into her own mind was any yardstick, then she supposed she must be smitten, too. Which only proved the foolishness of Nedda's notion.

Beth knew full well what Nick McCullough at times—all right, increasingly—could make her feel. And she was old enough, experienced enough, to put a name to it. Sexual attraction. It happened to people all the time and with all sorts of people. The world would be in a fine mess if everybody chose to act on those feelings every time they occurred.

But, all of that notwithstanding, Beth had become savvy enough in the ways of small towns not to share any of her thoughts about Nick with Nedda. Or, for that matter, any of the things she and Nick had discussed. Not that there'd be any point in mentioning them anyway. The case was closed. For her and—the stab of regret was as unexpected as it was disconcerting—after her blunt refusal last night, no doubt for Nick, too.

Chapter Seven

Two miserable and lonely days later, five minutes before closing time, Nick came into the diner.

Beth was bussing a table and had her back to the entrance when he entered. But even so, she knew the instant he set foot inside the door. Though nothing changed, no greetings were called out and the hum of conversation remained at the same level as before, some inner antenna she'd never known she had, alerted her to his presence.

A tingling awareness along the back of her neck, no more, was enough to snap her head around and drink in the sight of him. He looked wonderful. Cheeks more rugged than usual from the biting wind, he was a tall and commanding presence in his bulky sheepskin jacket with the collar turned up and the brim of his Stetson pulled low, shading eyes that had homed in on Beth like twin sapphire lasers.

Something elemental and powerful shifted inside Beth's chest. Her heart began to pound and her throat to close up. Desire was a hot, almost liquid snake writhing in the pit of her stomach, making her cheeks flush.

The glance they exchanged lasted only for a few heartbeats, but even in that short space of time, Beth had seen her own potent reaction mirrored in Nick's eyes. It further unnerved her, making her "Hi, Nick" come out in an embarrassing squeak.

She cleared her throat and managed to reduce to a decently professional level the smile she felt ready to burst forth.

"Take a seat." Thank goodness her voice sounded normal again. "I'll be right there to take your order."

She quickly finished her bussing, deposited the collection of dirty dishes into the tub under the counter and approached Nick, pad in hand. By now it was seven o'clock. The diner was due to close. But, of course, any customers already inside the door would not be denied service.

Nick had taken a seat in a booth, his only concession to being indoors the removal of his hat and unbuttoning of his coat. He wasn't hungry—not for food, anyway—and, after two sleepless nights, had already consumed enough coffee that day to give him a week of the jitters.

Or maybe it was Elizabeth. Knowing the taste and feel of her and all the time wanting her had his limbs twitching so he couldn't sit still and his gut feeling as if he'd swallowed a mess of grasshoppers. Certainly all of those unsettling symptoms had increased tenfold the minute he'd stepped foot in the diner and clapped eyes on her.

And, with her standing in front of him now, all rosy, flustered and as breathless as he, those symptoms increased another ten- or a hundredfold. He had it bad, but—boy, it felt good.

He grinned at her. Beth's heart did a crazy flip-flop and she grinned back. A happy, sappy kind of grin like Nick's that faded as their eye contact lengthened and neither of them spoke.

"I wasn't sure you'd ever want to see me again," Beth said finally. She had missed him terribly. She hadn't known that he—that anyone—could become so important to her in such a short time. It would hurt to leave him....

She pushed the thought aside. "I thought you might be mad at me."

"Mad?" Nick scoffed at the notion. "Hell, no. Takes more'n one stubborn female's refusal to see sense to make me mad. I've been busy."

Beth still hadn't asked for his order. Neither noticed or cared, but Nedda obviously did. Nick was the last remaining customer by now.

She hollered, "You plannin' to eat somethin', Nick? Charley wants to close up the kitchen."

Her raucous voice recalled Nick and Beth to the here and now. They exchanged rueful grins.

"No, Ned," Nick bellowed back, his gaze never leaving Beth's. "Go ahead and close up. I'm just here to take Elizabeth home."

Beth's eyebrows rose at the announcement, made in such a take-it-for-granted tone. But she didn't object. Truth was, she was too darned glad to have him back.

Nedda, sounding intrigued, pleased, drawled a thoughtful "Is that so?" before adding in her normal, strident tone, "Well, then stop wastin' her time so we can get crackin'!"

* * *

"Just so you know, I'm not here to pressure you" was the first thing Nick said to Beth when they were out on the sidewalk. "But I took the liberty of having my lawyer do some checking."

"Oh?" Side by side, head down against the wind that was stirring up snowdrifts and swirling crystals of snow that stung their faces like a thousand tiny needles, they crossed the street and hurried toward the rooming house. "Checking into what?"

"That thing you told me, about your dual citizenship. Your being able to just go to Canada and work there..."

"Oh?" Beth said again, and added a murmured "Thanks" when Nick held the door for her to enter the rooming house.

Inside the entry, she turned to face him. "Would you like to come up?"

"Do you want me to?"

Beth knew what she *didn't* want, namely to spend yet another evening with only herself and her worries for company. "I've got some wine," she offered tentatively. "I still owe you for the drink you bought at Starkey's, and you haven't told me yet what your lawyer found out. So..."

She waved a hand toward the stairs.

"Why, in that case, thank you, ma'am—" Nick gestured for Beth to precede him "—after you."

Her small room seemed even smaller with Nick in it. As they each shed their bulky outerwear, they bumped elbows twice. Beth was nervous suddenly. Nick's proximity brought memories of his kiss rushing back like a flood.

"Have a seat." Gesturing toward the one easy chair, she busied herself with glasses and wine. "I'm afraid all I have are these tumblers...."

"I don't mind." Nick stuck a finger inside his shirt collar and tugged. "Warm in here, isn't it?"

"Hmm." Actually, Beth had just been stifling a shiver. "Here you go." She handed him the glass, making sure their fingers didn't touch. "Cheers."

"Yeah." Nick drank, grimaced. "Dry. Good."

The obvious falsehood made Beth laugh and relax. "It's terrible and you know it." She set her own glass on the nightstand and perched on the edge of the bed. "So tell me what your lawyer uncovered that's so all-fired important."

"Did I say it was important?"

"No, but I figured it must be if it brought you to see me in this kind of weather."

Nick's eyes darkened and the tension between them was back. "It'd take a hell of a lot more than a bitty blizzard to keep me from comin' to see you, Elizabeth."

Beth couldn't tear her gaze from his. "Nick, please..."

"Yeah." Looking away with visible effort, Nick tossed back the remainder of his wine, got up and strode to the window.

"Seems you're only partially right in your assumptions, li'l Betsy," he said, his voice strained. "While it's true that you have claim to Canadian citizenship through your mother and that dual citizenship is possible for you, it's not something that automatically happens."

Beth stared at his back, anxiety beginning to knot up her stomach. "What're you saying?"

Nick turned. "I'm saying you have to *apply* for citizenship, Elizabeth. And that you won't be able to work in Canada and support yourself until citizenship has been granted."

"All right." Too agitated to sit, Beth paced. "So I'll apply right away...."

"The process takes months."

"But we can still live there, right?"

"Yes." Nick set his glass on the shelf by the wine bottle. "But two, or even three thousand dollars isn't gonna go very far. Elizabeth—"

"No, Nick." She didn't want to hear what she knew he wanted to say. "Please," she said. "Don't ask me again."

"It only makes sense." *I want you so much.*

But Beth shook her head. "Maybe to you. Not to me."

"You're scared."

Her small laugh was bitter. "The understatement of the century."

"But there's no reason to be." Nick wished he could tell Beth what was really in his heart, but, knowing she wasn't even remotely ready to hear him, settled for an emphatic "I...care about you, Elizabeth. And, dammit, woman, I know you care for me."

"Oh, Nick." Beth's eyes filled. "Don't you see that's all the more reason for me to be scared? I cared once before, and look what happened. I ended up barely alive and with my feelings trampled in the dirt."

"You can't compare me with *him,* Elizabeth."

"How can I not?" she cried. "Do I really know you?"

"Don't you?" Nick asked quietly. "Enough to know I'm different?"

Of course she knew. Instinctively, if nothing else. But instincts could be wrong. "I don't *dare* risk it again, Nick. So please don't ask me anymore."

"All right, Elizabeth." With a long exhalation, Nick tugged her into his arms and gently held her. "Relax, sweetheart. You win. I'll give you the money to go to Canada. However much it takes, it's yours."

Beth's head was still reeling as, about an hour later, she was getting ready for bed. Nick had left almost immediately after making his generous and astounding offer, staying only long enough to get into his coat and tell her to call if she should need him.

And Beth had moved in a daze ever since. She couldn't believe it. Thanks to Nick, it was now all there for her. She could go. She could fetch Jason and head for the Yukon by the end of the week at the latest. She should be happy. Delirious.

Beth stood by the window and looked out at the snow. So why did she feel as if she'd just lost her best friend?

Because it would sadden her to leave Starville, she told herself. She'd formed attachments here in spite of herself. Nedda, Charley and the other girls at the diner. They'd all been so good to her. She'd made a life of sorts for herself in this speck of a town, so of *course* it'd be painful to leave. Except for missing Jason, she'd been happier in Starville than she could remember being anywhere for a long, long time.

So why don't you stay, Elizabeth, in a place where you're happy and have friends? Why trade it for uncertainty and loneliness far away?

Because staying here is too risky. Jason will surely find us.

So marry Nick.

How simple that sounded. Beth turned away from the window and marched over to the bed. Marry Nick, indeed. She punched her pillow. At best, marriage was anything but simple, and at worst—

She had had the worst. It'd been hell, but she had survived. And Nick was nothing at all like J.C.

Frowning, Beth punched the pillow again.

Could it be that in not marrying Nick McCullough, she was cheating herself out of a shot at the best?

"Beth?" Her landlady's voice and accompanying rap on the door temporarily spared Beth from dealing with that startling question. "You still up?"

"Yes, I am." Beth hurried to open the door. "Myrna. Come on in."

"Thanks, but there's a phone call for you."

"A phone call?" Beth's heart froze. *Jason.* Something was wrong. Kathy was the only person to whom she'd given Myrna's private phone number. Strictly for emergencies.

"Oh my God." Almost tripping over herself, Beth rushed down the stairs to Myrna's out-of-date parlor.

"Kathy?" Beth gripped the old-fashioned black dial phone like a life line. "Kathy, what's wrong?"

"I'm not sure...." The slight huskiness and hesitation in Kathy's normally brisk and assertive speech made Beth's anxiety soar off the chart. "But I think it's—"

"J.C."

"Yes."

Beth closed her eyes and sank down onto the chair Myrna was pushing toward her. She bent her head into her hand. "Tell me."

"I was out tonight. A meeting—"

Beth's head snapped up. "He *came?*"

"No, no," Kathy hastened to assure her. "Nothing like that." An audible sigh. "I'm sorry, Beth. I'm afraid I'm neither handling nor telling this very well. It was a phone call. Mindy Simons, she's the fourteen-year-old who usually sits with Jason when I go out, took the call. She says a man asked for Katherine Grimes. She told him I was out and was there a message."

"And?"

"And he said no. There wasn't. Oh, Beth," she burst out. "He asked to speak to Jason!"

"What!"

"Mindy told him that Jason was asleep and asked the caller's name. But he'd already hung up."

"Sure." Enraged suddenly, Beth jumped to her feet. "After the damage is done, she asks for a name!"

"Beth—"

"What kind of incompetent baby-sitters are you hiring anyway, Katherine? I trusted you...."

"Beth—"

"If anything happens to Jason, so help me..." Beth's voice broke, her impotent rage cooled as rapidly as it had ignited. Too shaken to stand, she dropped back onto the chair. Her burning eyes fastened helplessly on Myrna who gazed back with a stricken expression.

"What're we going to do, Kath? What'll we *do?*"

"First off, we're not going to lose our heads." Kathy's tone was back to its no-nonsense self, no doubt due to Beth's emotional short circuit.

"It was J.C., Kath," Beth whispered. "I'm sure of it."

"Yes, well, I tend to agree. If not himself, then certainly someone he's hired."

"Do you think he's there?"

"Here in Brockton? No. It's too soon. The man hasn't been out of jail much more than a week, Beth."

"He's determined."

"Well, so am I." Kathy's voice rang with conviction. "We're not going to wait around—"

"Bring Jason to me, Kath."

"Right. So here's what I'll do. First light, I'll drive with Jason to my sisters in Rutland. There, just to be on the safe side, I'll switch cars and continue on to my parents' in Manchester. You can reach us there by tomorrow afternoon. We'll spend the night, and Thursday morning fly to Newark. Roger—"

"Your brother, the cop?"

"Right. He doesn't live too far from the airport and we'll bunk with him overnight before catching a plane out to Seattle Friday or Saturday. I'll see what I can get, reservationswise. Anyway, those are details we can talk about tomorrow. What do you say?"

"Thanks, Kath. What else can I say? You've been a brick. I'm sorry I fell apart...."

"Oh, shut up."

Beth smiled at her friend's gruff affection. She had herself in hand again, now that a course of action had been mapped out. "I'll set things up at this end. I—"

She hesitated, briefly wondering if she should mention Nick and, glancing at Myrna who was unabashedly—albeit sympathetically—eavesdropping, decided against it.

"I'll call you in Manchester," she said instead.

A little while later, after thanking Myrna and assuring the kindhearted woman that she'd be all right, Beth was back in her room, pacing.

Though far from all right, she felt calmer now. Composed. Kathy's plans were sound, as was her reasoning that J.C. couldn't possibly be, or have local contact, in Brockton so soon after his release. Whoever had made the phone call had done so long-distance. Which meant that by the time he did get there, even as soon as tomorrow, Kathy and Jason would be gone. J. C. Christofferson would be back on square one.

Only temporarily, to be sure, but long enough for Beth to put her own freshly hatched plan into effect.

She checked her watch. It was almost ten. Too late to call anyone?

In this case, Beth doubted it. Taking her jar of coins, she tiptoed down the stairs to the pay phone. As noiselessly as possible, she dropped a quarter into the slot and dialed.

One ring. She held her breath and rehearsed her speech. Two rings. Her heart raced. Three—

"McCullough."

Nick sounded gruff, preoccupied. Beth almost lost her nerve and hung up. But then she thought of Jason who was practically on his way over to...where? Her tiny room here at Myrna's?

No.

With a deep breath, her chin came up. "Nick," she said, proud of the fact that her voice shook only a little. "Will you marry me?"

Nick had wanted to come over but Beth stood firm on that score. They would work out the details tomorrow, she'd told him. And not until after the noontime rush at the diner.

In the end, with flattering reluctance, Nick had agreed to pick Beth up at two o'clock.

Arriving, the first thing Nick did was to rattle Beth, and delight Nedda and her diner full of customers, by sweeping Beth into his arms and kissing her soundly.

"They may's well know that you're mine now," he said complacently when Beth, still hot-faced and embarrassed, attempted to chide him on the way out to Triple Creek Ranch.

"In name only," Beth reminded him.

Nick brushed that aside. "We'll get to the details later."

The ranch house kitchen was immaculate, a far cry from the cluttered mess it had been Saturday night, after the party.

Nick hung their coats on a back door peg and tossed his hat onto another. Beth couldn't help but be charmed—and warmed—by his almost boyish high spirits.

"Want some coffee?" he asked.

"Sure, thanks."

"Know how to make it?"

Beth relaxed enough to grin at him. "You mean you don't?"

Nick tossed back a crooked grin of his own. "I mean I do, but don't particularly like to." He opened a cupboard and pointed. "There's the coffee. I figure, since this'll be your kitchen soon anyway, you might's well start making yourself at home."

He was right, of course, but his words gave Beth a peculiar little jolt. Washington was a community property state. Which meant that soon, all of this, this homey old log house, the outbuildings, the livestock, the ranch—*everything* would be half hers.

Unless Nick put some sort of financial proviso into that prenuptial agreement they'd talked about after the party.

Beth decided she would insist on it. She would never feel right, given the nature and circumstances of their marriage, to have claim to McCullough property.

Which didn't mean, however, that she couldn't make coffee and other things in this wonderful, spacious and well-equipped kitchen. It would be a pleasure, in fact. She'd always liked to cook; she had always liked to keep house, for that matter. She knew that probably made her old-fashioned—*boring,* was the way J.C. had put it—but she had always found the nurturing and caretaking of her family profoundly satisfying.

If her life had taken a different turn, if she'd married a different man...

Her gaze flew to where Nick was lounging in the doorway, watching her scoop coffee into the coffeemaker's basket as though it were the most fascinating thing he'd ever seen. Self-conscious, she quickly looked back at her task.

"There." Nervous now, she flipped the switch and turned to Nick with a too-bright smile. "In a few minutes you'll have your coffee. We might as well get to work while we're waiting, huh?"

"Sure." Nick pushed away from the door frame. "I worked out a preliminary draft of the agreement. Let me go get it. It's in the study."

By the time he came back with a yellow legal pad in hand, Beth had gone ahead and gotten two mugs out of the cupboard, opening a few doors before she found them and telling herself that was okay. She'd also found the cream and sugar, but knew from the diner that Nick drank his black. She didn't. She liked four spoonfuls of sugar, a fact which had Nick watching in horror as she spooned mounds of the white stuff into the dark brew.

"How do you keep your girlish figure, scarfing sugar like that?"

"By avoiding coffee whenever possible." Handing him his mug, Beth brought her own to the kitchen table and, catercorner to him, sat down. "I only drink about a cup or two a week."

Nick shook his head watching her stir. "That stuff's gotta be like syrup to drink."

"Here, want to try some?" Beth had offered without thinking, holding the mug out to him. By the time she realized what she was doing and wished she could renege, it was too late. Nick had already taken the cup out of her hand.

"Sure," he said, his eyes on hers and beginning to kindle. "Why not?"

Why not, indeed? Watching him watch her as he pursed his lips slightly and curled them around the rim of her mug, Beth knew darn well why not. It was sexy, that's why not. She knew it was crazy, knew that drinking from cups was about as mundane as any task could get, and yet the act of watching Nick McCullough sip from her cup stirred her more than J.C.'s most skillful foreplay had ever been able to do.

The realization brought a wave of heat to Beth's face which further unnerved her because it was the same as waving a banner at Nick that read You turn me on.

The light in his eyes and the peculiar little smile on his lips—bittersweet and almost...tender—left Beth with no doubt that he knew exactly what watching him had made her feel.

"Hmm," he said, his voice deep as he handed the mug back to her. "Sweet."

And as their gazes clung a moment longer, Beth was left with the unsettling impression that he hadn't meant the coffee.

"Yes," she said, severing eye contact and turning brisk. "That's the idea, of course." She straightened her spine and nodded toward the legal pad. "You said you had a draft? You've been busy."

"Yup." Nick pushed the pad toward her. "Whyn't you take a look at it? If you can read my chicken scratch."

"No problem."

"It's only a couple of sentences."

"I see that."

And still their gazes clung.

"I checked with the judge," Nick said. "It only takes three days in this state to get a marriage license. We can be married on Saturday."

Saturday. So soon. The beast of panic reared its ugly head. Beth took a deep breath and subdued it. Of course, so soon, dummy. Jason is coming. There's no time to lose if he's to have a home to come to.

"Saturday sounds fine."

Nick's eyes darkened. "I think it does, too."

"So..." Beth said, forcing her gaze onto the paper in her hand. "Ahem. Let's see what this says...."

Beth read, blindly at first, but then the words began to take shape. One sentence dealt with termination of the marriage after a year if either party desired it.

No problem with that. It was what she wanted, too.

The next stated: *Both parties agree to conduct themselves in public as any loving married couple would.*

She hesitated a moment on that one while her throat worked to swallow against a certain dryness. But then she thought, If it's important to Nick, why not? It shouldn't be too difficult....

The final proviso took a little longer to read and come to terms with. Beth read: *Elizabeth...blank... Coleman...*

"I didn't know what your middle name was," Nick said, watching her closely.

"It's Margret, after my other grandmother."

"Oh."

Beth read on. ...*agrees that Dominick Bronson McCullough—*

"Bronson. Is that a family name?"

"Yup. My mother's."

"Oh." Beth glanced down again. ...*be allowed to do everything in his power to persuade Elizabeth Coleman to assume the role of his wife in the fullest sense of the word.*

"Oh, my." Beth found it difficult to raise her eyes.

Until Nick said, "That part's not negotiable."

Then her head snapped up. "Now just a minute. I thought we agreed the marriage would be...wouldn't be—"

"And it won't," Nick said calmly. "Not until *you* want it to be."

"You make it sound as though it's just a matter of time."

"I'm hoping it will be—yes."

"Well, stop hoping," Beth flared. "It won't happen."

"Are you saying you can't stand me?"

"No, that's not what I'm saying, and you know it! I mean, I wouldn't have called you if that were the case. You know darn well it's marriage per se I can't stand!"

"And I say, how do you know? You've never had one."

"Never had one?" Nick was being so darned calm and collected, it was driving Beth crazy. They might as well be discussing the sale of some cattle for all the emotion he showed.

"No. What you had with Christofferson wasn't a marriage."

"But what you had with Susan was?" The moment the words were out, Beth wished she could call them back. Especially when Nick visibly flinched. What was the matter with her? Why was she acting this way toward a man who was only trying to help?

Her hand shot out to touch his. "I'm sorry...."

"That's all right." It had been a cheap shot, but Nick figured Beth was entitled. He had been pushing her, trying to sell her on this, to him, most crucial condition of their contract. He looked down at her hand, still covering his in a featherlike touch that he nevertheless felt right down to his toes. She withdrew and he sighed.

"And the answer is, no," he said heavily. "What Susan and I had wasn't violent, but it wasn't much of a marriage. And it was hell to me, just as yours was to you. But I do know of plenty of marriages that aren't that way and I bet you do, too."

Beth thought of her grandparents, of the obvious love they had shared even after forty years of marriage.

Nick leaned toward her, his expression intense. "*That's* the kind of marriage I want with you, Elizabeth."

"But..." She spluttered, troubled, scared, but just a little bit hopeful, too. "But there needs to be love for a marriage like that," she finally managed to say in a voice that was little more than a whisper.

"I know." Nick's callused palm cupped her cheek and his gaze dipped deeply into hers. "I'm banking that love will come."

"And—" Beth swallowed. The urge to nestle her face into his hand was almost overwhelming. "And if it doesn't?"

"Then after a year we're free to go our own way." Nick searched her eyes, touched by the fear and uncertainty there and vowing he would do his utmost to replace both with love lights for the rest of her days.

He longed to kiss her. His gaze dropped to her lips. As if he'd touched them with his tongue the way he wanted to do, they parted. Her heartbeat was speeding up; he could feel it with the tips of his fingers resting at her temple. He *was* able to move her. The knowledge speared him with joy.

He brought his head closer, so close their breaths mingled. "Deal?" he said in a rough whisper, his eyes still on her lips.

The tip of her tongue came out for a nervous lick. Nick's mouth went dry and he felt himself harden. It was all he could do not to crush her to him. And then those sweet lips of hers opened a little farther, and on a softly shuddering exhalation came the word he longed to hear. "Deal."

With a groan, his lips claimed hers in one deep, hard kiss that sealed the bargain.

Beth called Manchester, New Hampshire, from Nick's study, with him seated behind his desk and hanging on her every word. After filling Kathy in without going into the particulars of her upcoming and—especially from Kathy's point of view—rather hastily decided upon nuptials, Beth said they'd talk some more later and asked to speak to Jason.

While she waited for Kathy to get him, her eyes found Nick's and stayed there.

"Let me switch over to speaker phone," Nick suggested. "I'd like to hear him, too."

Beth agreed with a nod, saying, "Hello, darling," when Jason's high, little-boy voice came on the line. "How's the trip going so far?"

"Great! We're gonna go on a airplane tomorrow."

"And stay overnight with a real policeman," Beth said. "Did Aunt Kathy tell you?"

"Yep. I'll bet he'll let me see his gun," Jason bragged. He then added a more hesitant "Don't you think, Mom?"

Beth and Nick exchanged amused smiles. And Beth assured him, "I'm sure he will."

"Neat-o."

Beth rolled her eyes. "And did Aunt Kathy tell you where you're going after that?" Beth asked.

"Yeah." All of sudden, Jason sounded subdued. Unsure. He'd learned not to hope, not to expect. The knowledge was almost more than Beth could stand.

Nick took her hand and reassuringly squeezed it. His eyes on hers were steady and warm. She managed a grateful little smile. "Darling, I have wonderful news for you."

"Oh?"

How cautious he still sounded. It took an effort for Beth not to break down, to keep the cheer in her voice. "How would you like to come live on a ranch?" she asked. "A ranch with real horses, and cows and... and chickens and...?"

Catching her questioning inflection, Nick mouthed, "Pigs, too."

"And pigs," Beth said. "And tractors."

If she had expected jubilation, she was in for disappointment. Silence followed her enthusiastic recital. A long one during which could be heard some ragged breathing that was broken at last by a shakily whispered, "And you, Mom? Are you gonna be staying there, too?"

She did cry then and had to press a hand against her lips so Jason wouldn't hear. Her other hand was still in Nick's and its warm pressure steadied her sufficiently to manage a small laugh along with a playfully scolding, "Well, of *course* I'll be there, pickle face! Do you think I want to miss all the fun?"

"And guess what?" she went on. "Your, uh, your uncle Nick will be here, too."

She and Nick had agreed that might be the easiest appellation for the boy to deal with.

"I have an uncle Nick?"

"You do now," Beth said cheerfully. "It's his ranch we'll be living on."

"Forever?"

There was such wistfulness in Jason's voice. He wanted a secure, forever kind of home so badly after all the upheaval and trauma of the past couple of years.

Beth swallowed a new rush of tears and avoided Nick's expectant gaze. "Forever is a very long time, sweetiepie."

"Well, that's what I want."

"I know you do, sweetheart." Beth closed her eyes and prevaricated. "And everything's going to be fine."

"When am I coming?"

"In just a few days, darling. In fact, if you'll let me talk to Aunt Kath, I'll find out."

"Okay."

After a few more reassurances and endearments, Kathy came on the line. "He's all lit up like a firecracker," she said, chuckling. "I've never seen him like this."

Beth looked at Nick with brimming eyes. "He's happy," she said to Kathy, and to Nick mouthed a silent but fervent "Thank you."

* * *

The Starville High School's annual Christmas pageant and band concert was preceded by a potluck dinner. It obviously was a big event because it seemed to Beth everybody in town and a good many ranch families had turned out for it.

"Would you come with me?" Nick had asked her after all the details of their not-quite-conventional marriage had been settled to their mutual satisfaction.

"I'm expected to go along with some of the family," he'd explained. "I generally do every Christmas, and this year a couple of the nephews have parts in the play. They're my brother Maynard's boys. He's got three. He and Sophie couldn't make it to the party...."

He'd grinned his crooked grin, the one Beth always had a hard time resisting. "It'd be a great way for you to meet the family and for us to spring the news on them."

Beth wasn't too sure about that, but realizing it would have to be done, had thought the Christmas pageant with its inherent theme of peace and goodwill just might be the best setting, after all.

Maynard McCullough was a heavier, but less grizzled version of his older brother. Beth thought to herself that he wasn't as handsome, either, but his many laugh lines attested to a lighter spirit than Nick's.

Or maybe he'd just been spared Nick's unhappiness, being married to Sophie whom Beth liked on the spot.

The couple was tanned and glowing, having just returned from a two-week vacation in Hawaii. "The kids would've skinned us alive if we hadn't come back for the pageant."

"That's for sure," Sophie laughingly agreed with her husband. "They've all got parts. Anyway," she explained to Beth, "that's why you haven't seen us at the diner. Not that we stop there all that often when we do get to town."

"None of the other McCulloughs seem to, either," Beth said. "I met Christine and Chuck for the first time at Nick's party."

"'Course they're both teachers here at the high school," Sophie said, "and working during the day. Did Karen and Mike make it?"

Beth shook her head. "Something about not being able to get a baby-sitter out to their place in that awful snowstorm."

"You'll like Karen," Sophie said. "She's Nick's favorite, being the baby and all. Besides, he's the one who raised her. He and their grandmother raised all of them, I guess, after their parents died some twenty-five years ago. Karen had just turned five, Chris was eight and Maynard was fifteen."

"Oh, how awful." Knowing only too well what it was like to lose one's parents, Beth sent Nick a warmly sympathetic glance, which he was too busy to notice, however. He was deep in ranch talk with his brother.

"What happened?" she asked.

"Oh..." Sophie shrugged. "Some freak thing. A car accident. Black ice, or something like that."

She suddenly looked past Beth and waved. "Over here, you guys!"

Beth turned just in time to see Nick hugging a broadly smiling woman of about her own age—Karen, Beth surmised—and heartily clap the stocky, heavily freckled man with her on the shoulder. A girl and a boy somewhere around Jason's age were each hugging one of Nick's legs.

She watched him bend to them and swing the little girl up in the air till she squealed. Setting her back down on the ground, he affectionately tousled the boy's straw-colored mop of hair. His pleasure in his sister and her family still alight on his face, he turned toward Beth.

"Come here, Elizabeth. Meet Karen." He put a proprietary arm around Beth's shoulder. "And this is Mike Sweeney, Karen's husband and the father of these two rapscallions.

"Caitlin," he said to the little girl who had his—and her mother's—sky blue eyes and dark shock of hair. "This is Beth Coleman. She's a very special friend of mine."

"Hi."

"Hello, Caitlin." As Beth solemnly shook the suddenly shy little girl's hand and delighted in the gift of a slow, gap-toothed smile, Nick deflected startled and questioning glances from his siblings. They were visibly intrigued by the phraseology of his introduction. How special? he could all but hear them asking. For the moment, he was content to just give them his twisted half smile. They'd learn everything else after supper.

"And this Huck Finn lookalike is none other than Little Mike Sweeney," he said. "He's eight."

"I've got a boy who's eight years old, too," Beth told Little Mike.

"Oh?" Little Mike looked around. "So where is he?"

"He's back East right now," Nick replied before Beth could. "But he'll be here after next Sunday and he'll be staying with me at the ranch, so you be nice to him and show him around. He's a city kid."

The Sweeney ranch bordered the Triple Creek to the east, so that they were neighbors.

"Hey, cool!" little Mike exclaimed. "How long's he stayin'?"

"Quite a while."

"He gonna go to school with me?"

"Yup."

This time Beth, too, noted Nick's family's openly speculative glances. In fact, Karen's expression visibly cooled as she looked Beth up and down with narrowing eyes.

To her chagrin, feeling vaguely guilty of some nebulous misdeed, Beth felt herself flush. She became even more flustered when Nick quite openly hugged her to him and, when she glanced up at him, gave her a long, possessive and warmly intimate look.

"Here come the others," Sophie announced, and Beth had to stifle a groan. She wasn't sure she was up to meeting any more future in-laws.

The others turned out to be Sophie and Maynard's three boys, ranging in ages from twelve to sixteen, as well as Nick's sister Christine and her husband, Chuck Whitney.

They apologized for being late, blaming their tardiness on typical last-minute glitches regarding the after-dinner program. Beth was thankful that here, finally, was someone she'd already met and who'd liked her. Of course, that had been before she and Nick had agreed to get married. Beth feared that on learning of their plans, the Whitneys' welcoming warmth, too, would change to Maynard and Karen's now frosty reserve.

Only Sophie remained determinedly warm and cheerful, introducing her sons—Paul, Bronson and Jack—in descending order of age and then hustled everyone into the food line at the potluck buffet.

The meal was eaten amidst bursts of stilted conversation among the adults and typical adolescent and teenage ribbing among the kids. Though the food was varied and, according to everyone else, delicious, Beth couldn't get more than a forkful down her shut-tight throat and didn't taste any of what she did manage to swallow.

She dreaded the moment Nick would announce their wedding plans. She couldn't help but feel that his family would misinterpret the haste of their marriage. They'd probably see her as some greedy little golddigger who couldn't get her claws into Nick quickly enough. After all, she was a stranger who'd come to Starville barely a month ago and who worked as a waitress for a living. They'd never believe that she'd fallen head over heels with their brother....

And, of course, she hadn't.

And yet according to their contract, she was supposed to act as though she really were madly in love with Nick, meaning she couldn't divulge the real reason and circumstance of the relationship between herself and their brother. They were bound to think the worst of her.

Karen was looking daggers at her already, and Nick hadn't even said anything yet. Oh, no...

Nick was asking for everyone's attention. The moment had come. Beth bowed her head, keeping her eyes on the mess she'd made of her food while listlessly poking it with her fork. She dreaded the shock and dismay that was bound to follow Nick's announcement.

But then her head came up and she thought, No, dammit. She wasn't doing anything to be ashamed of. She and Nick knew what they were doing and that was all that mattered. Besides, even without love, she had every intention of making Nick as happy as she could, given their circumstances. She owed him that, and so much more.

Nick took Beth's hand in his. Instantly concerned because it was ice-cold, his gaze sought hers. "You all right?"

"Fine." Beth managed a reassuring little smile. Only he noticed that it wobbled around the edges. He squeezed her hand, and faced his siblings.

"Elizabeth and I are going to be married," he said and in the stunned silence that followed, looked at Beth with an expression so intense and so hot, it made her heart slam to a stop and her breath catch in her throat.

It was Sophie who found her voice first. Sitting next to Beth on the right, she gripped Beth's free hand in both of hers.

"Congratulations," she said with genuine warmth, smiling first at Beth and then at Nick. "I'm sure we'll all be great friends by the time the big day rolls around."

"T-thank you," Beth stammered, still shaken by Nick's look and warmed by Sophie's ready acceptance. She was just wondering if maybe she'd been wrong in her assessment of Nick's family, when Karen spoke up.

"So tell us, big brother," she said sweetly while, at the same time, raking Beth with a withering glare. "When's the *big day* going to be?"

"Saturday," he said, facing them all squarely and holding Beth's icy hand in a warm and reassuring grip.

With the noise of a gymnasium full of eating, talking and laughing people ebbing and swelling all around them, a pin dropping would have been heard at the McCullough family's trestle table, so profound was the shocked silence that followed Nick's calm words.

"This Saturday at Judge Selkirk's office in Spokane."

Chapter Eight

The remainder of the evening had not brought a lightening of the spirit to the assembled McCullough clan. After offering their cursory and reluctant felicitations—only doing so because Nick's authoritative glare dared them not to—everyone except Sophie and the little ones had proceeded to ignore Beth and to address Nick only when necessary.

They had all helped to clear the floor of the gym so the band could set up, and afterward had followed the crowd up into the bleachers. They had loudly applauded Paul McCullough's performance as Scrooge in this year's production of Dickens's *A Christmas Carol* and had sung along, as requested, with the band's closing rendition of "Silent Night."

And afterward they had rounded up their broods and bid a hasty good-night, leaving Nick and Beth to stroll out into the clear and frosty night at a more leisurely pace. Outside, they ran into Nedda and Frank and, with indulgent chuckles, the play as well as the band's not-always-stellar performance were rehashed for a few minutes. They waved and exchanged hellos with some others they knew as they walked up Main Street. And then they were alone and in front of the rooming house.

They turned to face each other. Beth, feeling battered and brittle, tried hard to summon up a smile. Nick didn't bother. His expression was as grim as she'd ever seen it. Beth wondered if, in light of his family's reaction, perhaps he'd like to change his mind. If so, she would certainly understand.

"Nick," she began, ready to tell him so, but Nick had started to speak at the same time she did, and she stopped.

"Look," he was saying, "I'm sorry," then stopped, too. "Go ahead," he said when neither spoke for a moment.

"Well." Beth, feeling awkward, sort of half shrugged. "I guess I was just anticipating what you were about to say. And, please, there's nothing to be sorry about. Really. I understand. I, I guess I knew all the time it wasn't such a good idea...."

"What wasn't?" Nick was staring at her as if she'd spoken Swahili. "What're you talkin' about?"

"Our agreement. It's obviously not going to work out. You saw how your family reacted. They—"

"They behaved like a bunch of jerks," Nick growled. "And believe me, they're going to hear about it."

He took a deep breath, touching a hand to her cheek. "I'm only sorry that your feelings were hurt."

"Oh, Nick." Beth impulsively held his hand in place. "Don't worry about me. I mean it's understandable, their being surprised and... and, well, *leery* of me. They love you and they don't want you hurt by some..." She shrugged, casting around for a fitting term. "Some *Jezebel* from God knows where...."

"Stop." Nick wasn't amused. In fact, he was furious with his siblings. They'd hurt Beth with their attitudes, and he was in no mood to be as understanding about it as she was trying to be.

Jezebel, hell! He was forty-five years old and he by damn knew a Jezebel when he saw one, and they damn well ought to know that. Elizabeth was a fine, decent woman and that ought to be obvious to them, too. They damn well ought to give him credit for good sense.

"Don't say another word," he told Beth. "And don't think for a minute that I've changed my mind or that I'm sorry. I'm not." He looked deeply into her eyes. His thumb stroked her temple. "You hear me, Elizabeth?"

Beth wordlessly nodded. She was overwhelmed by his gruff tenderness. All this just to get help for his housekeeper? she wondered, mesmerized by his burning gaze.

Nick wanted her. It was there in his eyes, hotly, boldly. He hadn't said so in explicit terms, but had certainly put her on notice with their contract's final clause. Once married, he would try to seduce her.

Thursday night—Beth's last night in Nedda's employ—after closing, everyone at the diner surprised her with a bridal shower. Sophie McCullough, came, too, but she was the only member of Nick's family who did.

Afterward, when Nick came to drive her and her belongings out to the ranch, she excitedly showed him all the gifts they'd received. They were pretty rather than the often strictly practical things that shower gifts so often tended to be. Things like vases, delicate figurines and, from Sophie, a sterling silver frame for their wedding picture.

"I didn't have the heart to tell her we wouldn't have one taken," Beth said to Nick.

He quirked a brow. "Who says we're not?"

"Well, it hardly seems right, given—"

"Right or not, we will have a picture."

Beth was to spend the night in the room that would be Jason's. Nick and Maynard used to share it as boys, Jeanie told her as she bustled around to straighten knickknacks already in perfect alignment and fluff already well-fluffed pillows, obviously in a state of joyous excitement.

A little while later, sitting with Nick in his study and sipping a nightcap—mint tea for Beth and a brandy for Nick—Beth thought it might be wise to clear up the matter of sleeping arrangements after the wedding. It was not a subject she was entirely comfortable broaching, especially given the fact that she seemed to be increasingly of two minds about how she'd like to see things progress.

"Nick," she said hesitantly, staring into the leaping flames in the fireplace and snugly ensconced in one of the two leather recliners that faced the huge, sandstone hearth. She liked the study much better than the large and somewhat impersonal living room and had thought to herself that if she were to live permanently in this house, that would be one room she'd dearly love to redecorate.

"Nick, uh, where will I sleep after we, uh, get back from Spokane? I mean—" she rushed on when Nick lazily turned his head to stare at her with a half-amused, half-indulgent expression on his face "—I mean, there's got to be another bedroom. One your sisters shared maybe. Or perhaps they each had their own rooms. I don't know. The point is, I could certainly sleep in one of—"

"You'll sleep with me in the master bedroom."

"What?" Lord, but she wished her voice hadn't chosen that moment to come out all squeaky. She sounded like a frightened mouse when what she really was was, well, indignant.

"Now look here..." She meant to tell him that that would be taking the third clause too far, but he interrupted.

"I see you've forgotten Clause Two," he said. "That's the one about acting the role of loving wife in front of others? Now what, for instance, would Jeanie think if you didn't sleep with me?"

"But Jean doesn't sleep in the house. She'd never have to know...."

"She'll know, Elizabeth. She's the housekeeper. Of course she'll know which beds have been slept in."

"All right," Beth said, not sure why she was arguing so hard when part of her thrilled at the thought of sharing the big bed with Nick in the master bedroom. Sharing it and—

She lopped off the thought. "So *I'll* take over that part of the housekeeping. After all, that *is* my part of this bargain. Having someone to take some of the load off Jean's shoulders *is* the reason you're marrying me in the first place."

No, it isn't, Nick thought, but didn't betray himself by even the flicker of a lash. All he said, and very reasonably, was "And my part of the bargain is to keep you safe. I can't do that when you're not with me."

"That's ridiculous," Beth flared. "It's not like I won't be right here in the house."

"Ah, but that's just it," Nick said. "You wouldn't be in the house. My sisters slept in what is now the guesthouse out back. You've seen it, the little place next door to Jean and Cy's. On the other side of the bunkhouse.

There are only two bedrooms in the main house, Elizabeth. Jason will be sleeping in one, which leaves the master bedroom for us."

"But—"

"Don't worry so much, li'l Betsy." Nick picked up her hand and laced his fingers through hers, his eyes keeping hers hostage. "You'll be perfectly safe from my baser intentions for as long as *you* want to be. Fair enough?"

After a moment of hesitation, and with her heart beating clear up in her throat, Beth nodded. "Fair enough. I, uh, I guess."

"Trust me?"

This time Beth didn't hesitate. "Yes," she said. "I do."

With their eyes locked, Nick brought her hand to his lips. "Thank you."

They left for Spokane the next morning. First stop, Nick's grandmother's house. Beth was to spend the night there, so Macie Donovan McCullough had decreed.

En route, Nick told Beth that he had confided the true circumstances of their wedding to his grandmother. He had never been able to lie to the old matriarch, he confessed. Every time he had, she'd seen through the lie and walloped the living daylights out of him.

He was too old to be walloped, he said with such an endearingly boyish grin, Beth felt her heart twist in her chest. And besides, he continued, Nan understood.

Beth didn't know what he meant by that until Nick went off to the prestigious old Belmont, the hotel where they were to spend their wedding night, but where Nick would be staying this prenuptial evening, as well.

Beth and Macie, who at eighty-six was still as sharp as a tack and very handsome, to boot, were finishing the last of their after-dinner port when the old woman said, "I was a mail-order bride, you know."

"You *were?*"

Visibly pleased by Beth's startled and intrigued reaction, Macie nodded. "Yup. Well, sort of, anyway. It was an arranged thing between my guardian, Sam Guthrie—I was an orphan, you see—and Dominick McCullough, Jr. He and Uncle Sam knew each other somehow—I forget the details. Anyways, that was nigh on seventy years ago. There weren't that many eligible females hereabouts. Sam'd seen to it I was properly raised and knew my way around a ranch. I was passing good-lookin' and didn't lack for brains, either, and so, when I was eighteen, they put me on the train and shipped me west."

"From where?" Beth asked, entranced by the old woman's tale.

"All the way from outside of Kalispell, Montana." She chuckled. "That might not seem like such a long way nowadays, but let me tell you, young lady, it was one high adventure for someone like me who hadn't been no farther from home than Kalispell. And with a man waiting for me at the other end, I don't mind telling you, I was a mite nervous."

She stopped to take a sip of her port. Holding the glass with her pinky extended, her eyes unfocused and dreamy, she stared into the distance. A small smile played at her lips and made her look young again.

"The first time I clapped eyes on your Nick's grandpa was when I got off the train in Spokane and there he was. So tall and hard. He looked much older than his twenty-four years. But, oh, he did look fine...."

Blinking, Macie recalled herself and, setting her glass down, patted Beth's hand. "The McCullough men are tough," she said. "Always were. But they're good men, too, ever' one. You'll be all right, with Nick there to look out for you. And now I'm tired."

She rose, and Beth stood, too. The two women looked at each other and then Macie said, "I'm a foolish old woman, I know, but I've always *loved* a good romance. I fell in love with my Nick, it didn't take but a few days of bein' his wife. Your Nick's his spittin' image. . . ."

She offered her cheek, wrinkled and fragrant with the vague scent of lilac. "You may kiss me good-night, dear."

Very carefully, and with an odd sense of homecoming, Beth did.

". . . I now pronounce you man and wife," the Honorable Judge Philip Selkirk said in conclusion, but Beth barely heard him. Throughout the brief, no-nonsense civil ceremony, she had hovered in a state that consisted in equal parts of a sense of suspended reality and stark terror. She wasn't sure what she was doing here, wasn't even sure with whom she was doing it.

As if caught in some strange kind of kaleidoscope, J.C.'s more youthful and sullen good looks superimposed themselves on Nick's manly and somber features, and she was transported back to that other, her first, wedding ceremony. For an instant, she felt again the excitement, the anticipation and even the love that the younger, and ever so much more naive Elizabeth Coleman had felt that day. But then she remembered the disappointment of her wedding night and the horrors of her marriage and went cold.

Panic gripped her. What was she doing, repeating the travesty? What was she letting herself in for here? Hadn't she learned the first time? Hadn't she promised herself, Never again?

She wanted to run. Adrenaline surged, and her body tensed in readiness. Her panicked gaze flew to the man beside her. He caught the look in his steady regard and held it.

Looking at him, reading reassurance and understanding in the clear blue of his eyes, little by little, Beth felt herself relax.

It'll be all right, Nick's gaze seemed to say. We can work it out. Together.

And Beth believed him. With a wobbly smile, she thought, Yes. Yes, we can. Together.

"Dominick McCullough, you may kiss the bride," the judge said at the same time as Macie poked her grandson in the ribs with the handle of her intricately carved walking stick. The poke rudely startled him out of his absorbed contemplation of his new wife's brimming eyes.

I love you.

How much Nick wanted to tell Beth the words that were in his heart. On his tongue. But he didn't, knew he couldn't. Not until he sensed in her the birth of some equally tender emotion. Oh, he knew that she was drawn to him, though, granted, sometimes more so than others. And he felt fairly certain that he could make her want him as he wanted her—abidingly, hungrily. Completely?

In his case, yes, that's how he wanted her. Completely. Not just her body, but all of her, heart and soul. But it would take a while for Beth to want him that way, too. She'd have to love him first, as he loved her.

Gazing into her eyes, he saw tears, yes, but none of the old sorrow that had shadowed them for so long. And he promised himself that he would cherish and protect her, and make her forget the past.

Slowly, reverently, he put his mouth on hers for their first kiss as man and wife.

There followed champagne and a sumptuous supper in the Belmont Hotel dining room. Nick's grandmother, the judge and his wife, Camille, who, along with Macie McCullough had acted as witnesses to the marriage, were the only guests. They tactfully departed soon after dessert, leaving the bridal couple to linger over their espressos.

Crossing the lobby a little while later, the strains of some lively dance music could be heard coming from the bar. Without a word, and without giving Beth a chance to protest, Nick steered her toward the sound and onto the crowded dance floor.

"A wedding dance," he murmured as he drew Beth into his arms. "It's tradition."

Beth had no idea what kind of dance they were dancing. It was a slow one, and with Nick leading her with a surprising amount of grace, given the limp that was his legacy from the plane crash, all she had to do was follow his moves. He was holding her close, so close, their legs and bodies touched with each twirl and step. But it wasn't a sexual, threatening kind of closeness, and so Beth relaxed and simply enjoyed.

She enjoyed the feel of Nick's cheek against her temple. She thrilled to the warmth of his palm against her back and felt comforted by the strength of his arm, holding her.

Closing her eyes, she relaxed more fully against his support and gave herself up to the beat of the music, the magic of the moment and the man with whom she shared it.

As if sensing her surrender, Nick drew her closer. Beth gladly followed until they were chest to chest, hip to hip. With each step, her inner thigh brushed against Nick's in a way that clearly defined the differences in their anatomy. She was woman. Nick was man. All man. Virile man.

Beth blushed as the proof of his virility was imprinted on her senses. She pulled away a little and sought his eyes. They burned into hers, their message as blatant and stirring as, seconds before, the feel of his arousal had been.

And then he stopped dancing and kissed her. Right there on the dance floor, right there in the middle of the partying crowd. He kissed her with passion, with hunger, with need. He kissed her deeply, longingly, his tongue smooth as silk as it captured hers and stroked back and forth. He kissed her the way a man kisses a woman when he wants her, needs her, in a way that didn't allow Beth any other response but to kiss him back.

And she wanted to. Right then, at that moment, she wanted to kiss and be kissed with a desperation and need the like of which she had never experienced. She wanted to press herself into him, be absorbed by him and absorb his strength in return. She ached to feel him, touch him, taste him the way a starving person craves the life-giving sustenance of food and drink. She pressed against him, clasped him tight, and for the length of this one wonderful kiss she was his.

And then it was over. Amidst cheers and applause, Nick lifted his head and stepped back. The band struck up a lively, foot-stomping tune and, with an endearing look of self-deprecation, Nick said, "I guess I'll sit this one out."

"Me, too," Beth said and, as all around them couples twirled and leapt around the dance floor, she took her husband by the hand and led him out of the bar.

Through the lobby they went, hand in hand, and, alone in the elevator, they stood close, regarding each other with smiles that were gradually replaced by an increasingly electric tension that made the air between them seem to hum.

"You're beautiful."

Beth heard the words, but, more than that, she heard the husky heat with which Nick uttered them. His gaze and the words were like a caress so alluring and tender, goose bumps erupted all over her body.

"Oh, Nick... Thank you." Without thinking, she raised on tiptoe and kissed his mouth. "You've been so good to me."

"Hush." Nick's arms came around her and kept her firmly in the cradle of his thighs, spread apart in a bracing stance. His mouth caught hers in another soul-stirring kiss just as the elevator stopped and the doors opened.

Without breaking the kiss, Nick swung Beth up into his arms and carried her down the hall. Her arms were tightly wrapped around his neck and the ardor with which she was kissing him back had him panting with hunger and need. Holding her easily with one hand, he fumbled in his pocket for the key and unlocked the door. He carried her over the threshold and, once inside the room, kicked the door shut.

Their mouths still joined, he crossed the room, walked through another door and over to the bed. Bracing himself on one knee, he bent and gently laid Beth on the mattress. She moaned as they continued to kiss and, when he made to lift his head and end the kiss, tightened her grip around his neck.

"No..." she whispered against his lips. "Stay... Kiss me some more...."

"Elizabeth..." This was tender torture. Nick wanted nothing more than to give into her plea, to accept the invitation of her body, arching now to meet his as he allowed the persistent tug of her arms to pull him down, down, until he lay on the bed next to her.

"Love me, Nick," Beth murmured, her hands in his hair now, stroking his head and drawing his mouth into the curve of her neck.

Kissing her there, inhaling the heady scent of her, tasting her with tongue and lips, Nick's senses reeled. His body screamed to possess her, to take what she offered. One leg lifted and covered her. She moved and his leg found a home between her thighs. She moved again, against him and then with him as, unable to help himself, Nick's hips responded to her blatant invitation to the mating dance.

"You're so good to me, Nick," Beth whispered, her arms spanning his torso, drawing him more fully on top of her. Her hands feathered across his back and down, lower, until they rested on his buttocks.

Nick felt himself slipping, felt the thread of his control stretch nearly to the breaking point. He loved this woman. He wanted her, desperately. Now and forever. She wanted him, too. Every touch, every move, every word she uttered made that clear. So she didn't yet love him. She was a grown woman. They were both consenting adults. Surely it'd be all right if—

"You're so good," Beth was saying, her voice choked and husky, her hands stroking and kneading his sensitized body into a near frenzy of need. "I want to make it up to you, Nick. Let me. Please. Let me show you how very grateful—"

Grateful!

A cold bucket of water couldn't have more effectively cooled Nick's ardor than that one word. His head shot up, his eyes sought hers. Fury and self-loathing slammed into his gut when he saw that she was crying. Had been crying all along, if the wetness of her cheeks was anything to go by.

With a violent, barely stifled oath, he surged off the bed and stared down at her. "Is *that* what this is about? Gratitude?"

Beth closed her eyes and averted her face against the blaze of emotion in Nick's expression.

"You think you owe me something and so you're willing to prostitute yourself—"

"No!" Shock brought Beth upright and widened her eyes. "No, Nick. It isn't like that. I really wanted—"

"Don't, Beth." Only weariness was left now in Nick's tone and expression. Weariness and an odd sort of tenderness. He bent and brushed at her tears with his thumb.

"Nick..."

"No." His thumb smoothed across her lips and silenced her. "I lost my head there for a while and maybe you did, too. I'd like to think you did, anyway, because the alternative is too ugly."

His gaze sought hers and held it. "I don't want there to be ugliness between us, Elizabeth. I don't want there to be pretense. I want honesty. Honest emotions. When and if you're ready to share those with me, we'll talk again. Meanwhile..."

He smiled into her eyes, his thumb a gentle pressure at the corner of her mouth until her lips parted. Nick's gaze shifted to observe the small movement, then lifted again to hers as he gently bestowed a kiss and straightened.

"Good night, Elizabeth." He turned toward the door, but not the one leading out into the hall.

"Where are you going?" Beth asked, bewildered. She had taken no notice of her surroundings as Nick had carried her in here. Were they in a suite? Did he intend to sleep on a sofa? She was on a king-size bed, same as she would be sharing with him back at the ranch....

She hurried after him. "Please, Nick, you don't have to leave...."

"I'm not going far, Elizabeth. My bedroom's right through this door." A wry smile accompanied his words. "With no Jean to keep tabs on us, I thought you might appreciate one last night of solitude."

"Nick..." Beth's throat closed up, his thoughtfulness making her behavior of moments ago seem crass and unfeeling.

"I'm s-sorry," she finally managed to squeeze out. "About the way I acted— No please, Nick, let me say this," she said quickly when Nick waved her apology away. "Because it wasn't just...gratitude. I really do—"

"Shh." He dropped a quick kiss on her lips. "Let's just leave it for now and get some rest. All right?"

Beth's nod was reluctant, because she wanted desperately to explain her confused emotions, perhaps as much to herself as to him. But she realized it might be better, for now, to let him have some space.

"G'night, Nick."

"I'll see you in the morning," Nick said, striding through the connecting door and closing it softly behind him.

Chapter Nine

En route to the airport next morning, Beth was a bundle of nerves. Not that she'd been in much better shape through the night and at breakfast. She hadn't. Too much had happened over the past few days to allow for emotional tranquillity of any kind. Her state of nerves was way too precarious to let her relax, never mind rest.

There was the knowledge that J.C. was out there somewhere and bound to be up to no good. There was Jason's arrival—the joy of it as well as the fear. How to tell him that she and Nick were married? How would he take having to share his mother with a man again? What if he didn't like Nick? What if Nick didn't like him? What if Jason had changed in the time they'd been apart? What if, God forbid, J.C. had somehow managed to find the boy and—

The what-if's were killing her.

And as if all of that weren't enough to give a person a case of insomnia as well as tongue-tied, hand-wringing anxiety, there was the marriage and all its attendant and unexpected emotional trauma. For instance, such as Nick's family's mixed reaction to its taking place, and their suspicion of her motives. And Nick's grandmother, so gracious and welcoming even though she knew the true nature of Beth and her grandson's union.

And there was Nick. Such a friend to her and—she'd tried to deny it, but no longer could—rapidly coming to mean so very much more.

She'd been self-conscious about seeing him this morning but he had put her at ease with his usual attitude of gruff matter-of-factness. He hadn't tried to kiss her—Beth told herself she was relieved—nor had he acted differently, as in *husbandly,* in any way. He'd been courteous, and solicitous about her lack of appetite, but otherwise taciturn.

Sitting beside him now as they drove to the airport with each of them wrapped in their own mantle of silence, Beth cast a glance at him and wondered what he was thinking. He looked quite forbidding with his brow lowered and his lips sternly compressed. It occurred to her that he, too, might be nervous about Jason's arrival.

As much to divert him as herself, she began to talk.

"You know," she said musingly, resting her temple against the back of her seat and looking past Nick out of his side window, "the weather was just like this the day Jason was born. Bitter cold and frosty. It was February twenty-fifth. There was snow in the forecast. I was alone when my water broke. J.C. was on a road trip with the team. Grampa had died the end of December."

The corners of her mouth turned down on a wistful sigh. "I was scared because I needed someone and there was no one there."

Nick lightly laid a hand on hers. "From now on, there always will be."

She thanked him with her eyes, though she wasn't convinced it would be so. After all, once their year was up, odds were she'd be on her own once again. But she didn't tell him that, only went on with her tale as if he hadn't spoken.

"The housekeeper, Anna, ended up driving me to the hospital. She was a nice woman. She stayed with me and held my hand for as long as they let her and she was still there after Jason was born. Later, Anna used to help me with him and baby-sit him. The baby adored her and she became my friend."

Beth fell silent a minute, her thoughts far away, and then she said, "As soon as J.C. realized that, he fired her and forbade me to have anything more to do with her."

Nick mumbled something harsh and succinct.

"He was jealous," Beth said. "Insanely so. He wouldn't let anybody get close to Jason and me, emotionally, I mean. After Anna, housekeepers came and went so fast, we hardly learned their names, never mind becoming friendly. Sitters were hired only through an agency and never the same one twice. Later, Jason was not allowed to go to preschool and, when he entered kindergarten, was not allowed to bring home friends. With J.C. away much of the time, *I* was the only constant in Jason's life, and even *that* J.C. resented and would've changed if he could have figured out how. Since he couldn't—" Beth shrugged "—he punished us. In time, Jason became petrified of his father and, and frightened of other men, too."

She refocused on Nick's face and fell silent.

After a moment, Nick glanced at her inquiringly. "What are you telling me, Elizabeth? That your son will be scared of me?"

"I'm saying he might be, Nick. And I'm trying to make you see why so you won't take it personally. He desperately needs a positive male role model, but it might not be easy to win his trust."

"I'll do my best." Nick's voice was gruff, but his eyes touched warmly on hers. "Don't worry so much."

The gate area was nearly deserted. Only a few people were there to await the incoming commuter flight from Seattle. It was Sunday; the flights primarily served the business travelers who were home already with their families. A young mother chased her squealing toddler, scooped him up and proudly introduced him to the beaming grandparents who arrived moments before a petite blond woman in jeans and a bulky fisherman's sweater emerged from the Jetway. A backpack was slung over one shoulder, another hung from her hand. Her other hand was tightly clutched by a wide-eyed, tousle-headed boy.

Nick knew who he was even before he saw Beth speeding toward the child with a strangled exclamation.

"Jason...!" Arms wide, she dropped to her knees as Jason let go of his companion's hand and launched himself against his mom.

Watching the teary reunion, Nick's throat closed up and his eyes misted. He had to clear his throat a couple of times as he approached the blonde so that he could speak. "Miz Grimes?" he asked, and when she nodded, said, "I'm Dominick McCullough."

He held out his hand which Kathy, her own eyes moist with emotion, accepted with hearty pressure. She was small, Nick thought, but she was wiry.

"A real pleasure to meet you, Mr. McCullough."

Nick liked her immediately. "Name's Nick, ma'am."

"And I'm—"

"Kathy! Thank you. Thank you." Carrying Jason in her arms as if he were three instead of eight, Beth rushed up to her friend and another teary hugging session ensued. Caught in the middle, Jason's eyes veered toward Nick.

Nick was struck by the somber earnestness with which the boy studied him. Elizabeth used to look at the world just as somberly when first they'd met. Nick vowed then and there that he'd do his damnedest to banish the boy's shadows as surely as he'd helped to banish Beth's.

The women parted with sheepishly happy smiles and kisses on Jason's cheeks and then Beth, still clutching her son, turned to face Nick. "Dominick..."

Nick had never seen her look more beautiful. Dissolved by emotion, but glowing with love, the sight of her made his breath catch. Just so she would look at him one day, he promised himself. All soft and pink with loving. Only, the loving would be for *him* then, for him as well as the boy.

Catching the eagerness in her eyes, one corner of his mouth lifted in his characteristic half smile. "Yes, Elizabeth?"

"Nick, this is Jason."

Nick's crooked smile deepened. "I kinda figured it might be. Hi-ya, Jase." He held out the large stuffed cougar he'd bought at the gift shop. "Welcome to cougar country."

Jason accepted the toy and solemnly eyed first it and then Nick. "What does that mean?"

"Means you're at the home of the Washington State University Cougars, that's what. You like football, son?"

Jason shrugged. "I dunno...."

"Haven't watched it much, huh?"

Jason shook his head, his expression uncertain. "Are you my uncle?"

"Well..."

"Becky Fisher says uncles have to be your dad's brother or your mom's brother. Are you my mom's brother?"

"Uh...no, son. No, I'm not. Matter of fact—"

"Gosh, you've gotten heavy!" Beth exclaimed brightly, setting Jason down with a quick but meaningful glance at Nick. This was neither the time nor the place to go into explanations about relationships, her look said. Straightening, she fanned herself to cool the fire Jason's pointed questions had brought to her cheeks. "Kathy, what've you been feeding this boy? He's grown so big."

Taking Jason's hand and tugging him along, she began to walk toward baggage claim, chatting a mile a minute as if she feared a lull would produce more awkward questions. Jason had no idea that she and Nick were married. Unless Kathy had mentioned it...?

Tossing a glance at her friend who was walking behind her with Nick, she saw that Nick had relieved Kathy of the two backpacks and that they seemed deep in conversation. The sight of Nick, even more rugged and imposing next to her friend's petite paleness, caused Beth's heart to trip. This man was hers, she thought with a sense of wonder. Legally, yes, and in every other way, too.

Should she want him.

It became increasingly difficult to remember the reasons why she shouldn't.

"So is Nick my father's brother, Mom?" Jason asked the minute Beth stopped talking.

Maybe this *was* as good a time as any, Beth thought resignedly. She said, "No, darling. As a matter of fact, he—"

"Goody," Jason interrupted her to exclaim and broke Beth's heart when he added darkly, "'cause I sure wouldn't like him if he were related to Dad."

But then Jason visibly cheered and half turned toward Nick, dragging his feet to slow his mother down. "So do you really have horses, Uncle Nick?"

"Yep." Nick came abreast of the boy who promptly handed the stuffed cougar to his mother and reached for Nick's hand. Nick felt as if he'd just been given a precious gift.

"Got cows, too," he said, his voice rough with new emotions.

"Can I ride one?"

"What, a cow?"

That made Jason giggle and earned Nick such a glowing glance from Beth, it warmed him right down to his toes.

"Nooo," the little boy said with a reprimanding tug at Nick's hand. "People don't ride cows, silly. They milk them."

"That's true enough," Nick agreed earnestly, "as far as that goes. In rodeos, though, cowboys do sometimes ride 'em as well."

"Really? Can I see it? When? What's a rodeo, anyway?"

They reached the luggage carousel amid Jason's excited questions, and when Nick went to retrieve their bags off the belt, Jason was right there with him.

"And I was worried he'd be shy with Nick," Beth said to Kathy.

"He's come a long way," Kathy said. "My neighbor, Jack Benson, is a really great guy. He and his wife have a daughter, Rachel, who's the same age as Jason. He spent a lot of time at the Bensons' playing with her. Jack took a real interest in him, too."

"That's wonderful." Beth hugged her friend's arm. "How can I ever thank you for—"

"Don't, Beth," Kathy interrupted. "I've loved having Jason stay with me. I'm really gonna miss him. . . ."

"Once this is all over, we'll come and visit," Beth promised.

"*Will* it ever be over, Beth?"

"God, I hope so." Beth hesitated, almost afraid to ask. "Did you...I mean, any trace of, you know...*him* along the way?"

"No," Kathy assured her. "I'm sure it's okay."

"Lord, I hope so." Beth cast a quick look around, unable to relax in this public place. "I worry."

"I don't blame you. But, surely, with Nick in the picture..."

"Yes." Beth looked at her friend. "What do you think of him?"

"He seems like a very nice man."

"Oh, he *is*."

The women smiled at each other. "I'm glad for you," Kathy said. "You deserve some happiness."

"Thank you." Impulsively, they hugged.

"How long can you stay?" Beth asked a little while later, as they trailed Nick, Jason and the luggage cart out of the terminal.

"Like I told you on the phone, I've got to head back tomorrow."

"Oh, Kathy."

"I know." Kathy, too, sounded regretful. "You know I would've loved to accept Nick's invitation to stay over the holidays, but I just can't. Aside from the deadline I mentioned before, I've got to be with Mother for Christmas or she'll throw a tantrum and make Daddy sick all over again. You know how she gets."

"Yeah, I know." Beth sighed. "Well, at least we've got tonight. Nick's grandmother has invited us all to dinner."

Macie McCullough had done herself proud. Right from the start it was as if they'd all known each other forever. Kathy had been charmed and Jason delighted to have a granny as well as an uncle. It had been nearly midnight by the time Beth, Nick, Jason and Kathy had trooped into the Belmont for some much-needed rest. In fact, Jason had fallen asleep in the car and Nick had had to carry him up to their suite. It was a chore he had gladly undertaken, touched as he was by the trusting way the boy had tucked his head beneath his chin and wound his arms around his neck.

They'd seen Kathy off at the airport and now they were almost at the ranch. Almost home. Beth marveled at how right it sounded when Nick said those words. Listening to Jason chatter on and on as if he'd saved up all his questions and ideas until he could finally spill them to Nick, Beth thanked God for giving her both, the boy and the man. She felt as if they really were a family, as if they'd been one forever. And she wished, again, that she could have married a man like Dominick McCullough in the first place so that Jason really could have had the kind of father he and every child deserved. A father like Nick.

She shot him a warm glance and blushed when Nick intercepted it. Behind them in the back seat, Jason had succumbed to the rigors of a late night and jet lag. He slept.

Nick's gaze stayed on Beth's. "Happy now?" he murmured.

"Very." Without thinking, Beth leaned toward him, laying a hand on his thigh. "Thank you, Nick. Thank you for everything."

Suddenly aware of the intimate placement of her hand and the tingling feel of Nick's lean and muscular thigh, Beth would have snatched her hand back had not Nick covered it with his and held it in place.

"Stay," he said quietly. "I like it when you touch me, Elizabeth. You might have noticed that the McCulloughs are a family of touchers."

Beth had not only noticed it, she'd been on the receiving end of quite a few hugs and pats from Nick's grandmother these past couple of days. Still, that kind of affectionate touching was not quite the same as what she was doing here.

Her high color must have told Nick what she was thinking because he slanted her an amused look. "I'm your husband, Elizabeth. You're my wife. Touching comes with the territory."

"Not necessarily," Beth said, but the prim tone she strove for was spoiled by the husky catch in her voice. "We have an agreement...."

"One I'm all for breaking just as soon as possible," Nick countered, and chuckled when Beth's face got redder. "Relax, sweetheart," he murmured, turning the car into the long drive leading up to the ranch house. "Remember, *you* get to set the pace."

He gave her a long, smoldering look that had every nerve in Beth's body going *ping!* "Only know that I'm ready and waiting...."

It was amazing to Beth how quickly and easily Jason settled into his new life. With only a few more days till the holidays, school was out, leaving Jason with plenty of time in which to become Nick's shadow. Man and boy were constantly together and, by the looks of it, neither would have wanted it any other way.

Beth might have been jealous—after all, *she'd* always been the center of Jason's life before this—if she hadn't been so thrilled to see her son unfold and blossom in a way she never could have accomplished on her own. Jason needed a man, a father, and it was perfectly obvious that Nick was not only willing, but eminently capable of being precisely what the little boy needed.

In the act of putting together a lasagna—Jean and Cy had given in to Beth and Nick's urgings and gone to visit their grandkids for Christmas—Beth watched Nick and Jason cross the yard toward the barn that housed the horses. The sight of them made her heart expand and her lips smile. They were decked out in identical outfits of sheepskin jacket, jeans, cowboy boots and Stetsons—Jason had been completely outfitted at Mueller's the day after they'd come home. Now he refused to wear any of his other clothes and was doing his best to imitate Nick's posture and gait right down to the slight limp. To an outside observer, they easily could be father and son.

And how well Nick played the part of the father, Beth thought warmly. As well as he played the part of husband, come to think of that. She thought of the little acts of kindness and consideration he performed with such matter-of-factness, and knew it wasn't a temporary act. He was a good man, genuinely good. A man who invariably complimented her on her meals and quite naturally helped to clear the table afterward. A man who, without being asked, would grab the other end of their king-size bedspread when she made the bed in the morning, and he never failed to ask if she needed anything from town when he went into Starville.

In the evenings, too, he was ever the thoughtful husband. He liked it when she came to sit in his den, reading while he worked on the books or caught up on correspondence. Or they just talked. Nick would discuss ranch-related problems with her, actively soliciting her input. He'd even gone so far as to discuss his finances, just as if she were a real wife and a proper partner instead of just a cause he'd taken on.

When Beth had pointed that out, he'd looked genuinely surprised. "You *are* my real wife," he had said. "And for as long as we're together, ours *is* a real marriage. The law says so, but, more importantly, *I* want it to be. Don't you?"

Beth had hedged, feeling uncomfortable, feeling as if Nick were doing all the giving while all she did was take.

"How can I ever repay you for all this?" she asked with real despair. "What are you getting out of this arrangement?"

"More than you can possibly imagine," he had said in a voice that vibrated with the strength of his emotions. "More than I ever dreamed I would have."

"But why?" Beth had cried. "How? Are you telling me there aren't women out there who'd give their eye teeth to marry a man like you?"

"Oh, I'd guess there are, sure."

"Women who'd gladly give you children, Nick," she'd frantically insisted. "Women who would love you and give you the son of your own you want and should have. Why are you wasting your time with me when you could have so much more?"

Her despair had brought him to where she sat by the fire. He'd leaned down to her and framed her face with his hands.

"I've got everything I want right here and now, Elizabeth," he had told her, and the huskiness of his tone had shivers chasing each other down her spine. "If things between us never got any better, I'd be content to have it so. But they're gonna get better, aren't they, honey?" He kissed her gently. "Soon, I think."

Soon.

Nick and Jason had disappeared inside the barn and Beth tried to redirect her attention back to the lasagna. But the word *soon* kept echoing in her head and her blood quickened as she remembered the previous night.

For the first couple of nights she'd managed to stay on her side of the huge bed she shared with Nick and he, too, had honored the invisible wall that divided the bed down the middle. Since they each had their own down comforter it was fairly easy to maintain an illusion of separate beds and avoid any accidental touching.

But last night she'd slept restlessly. She had gone to bed before Nick. As usual, he was giving her all the time and privacy she needed for her nightly bath and bedtime rituals.

Generally, she was still awake when he came in to get the pajamas he'd told her he'd bought, and wore, strictly for her benefit, and took them into the bathroom with him. He'd come to bed then, smelling of soap and looking heart-stoppingly virile even in tailored pajamas, and they'd companionably read for a while or watch some late-night talk show on the bedroom TV.

Nick was like a roommate, Beth had told herself. He was every bit as easy to live with as Kathy Grimes had been back in college.

Except for the fact that he was a man.

Which was a fact that, increasingly and to Beth's intense discomfort, became more and more difficult to overlook. With every day they interacted, with every evening they spent in on-and-off conversation in his den, with every night she shared the same mattress and inhaled his clean, male essence, Beth became more aware of him, more drawn to him.

And that much closer to falling in love.

It frightened her even as it thrilled her, even as she told herself that falling in love with Dominick McCullough would be nothing at all like falling in love with J. C. Christofferson.

She had been young then. So young. At twenty-one, raised by grandparents and taught by nuns, she'd been terribly naive and younger than her years. She had been dazzled by J.C's dark good looks and burgeoning celebrity status. She'd been flattered to be noticed by him. Wanted by him.

Not given to sharing his thoughts and feelings, J.C. had been a stranger, even after four months of courtship. It had added to the mystique of him. But he remained a stranger for all of the ten years of their marriage, too.

So had she been in love?

Looking back on it all from her vantage point of bitter experience and hard-won maturity, Beth knew she never had been.

She had never felt the warmth of sharing she felt with Nick. She'd never delighted in watching J.C. do mundane chores the way she did when watching Nick. She'd never felt as cherished and protected as Nick made her feel merely by being in the same room or knowing he was nearby. And she'd never experienced this melting, churning heat, a heat that roiled in the pit of her stomach and made her breath catch, in all the times she'd seen J.C. in the nude. Well, looking at Nick McCullough fully clothed made her feel just that.

Where Nick had a quiet strength that soothed and reassured, J.C. had been a raw and violent power that riled and threatened. He had been a powder keg of emotions that were all the more bewildering since he'd never bothered to explain himself in any way.

And last night, in Beth's dream, the powder keg had exploded, just as it had so many times in the waking nightmare her life used to be.

She'd come awake kicking and fighting against some powerful restraint that wouldn't let her run, wouldn't let her escape from the punishment J.C. would mete out if he caught her.

"Noooo! Pleeeaase . . . !"

"Elizabeth." Nick's concerned voice finally penetrated.

"Nick?"

"That's right, sweetheart. I'm right here. Everything's fine. Hush now, I've got you. . . ."

Boy, did he. Gradually coming fully awake, Beth had found herself practically nose to nose with her in name-only husband. Much more disturbing than that, however, was the dawning awareness that other, more intimate parts of her were much, much closer than their noses. They were chest to chest, belly to belly, and one of her legs was firmly wedged between both of his. Their pajamas were no barrier when it came to feeling his heat and steely strength.

Because wanting to stay was the first impulse, Beth immediately began to struggle for release. "Please, Nick, let me go...."

"Hush." He lightly kissed her lips to silence her. "You're still upset. You had a dream. Let me hold you."

"Nick, you promised."

"I never promised not to hold you." He brushed his cheek against hers. The slightly abrasive caress stroked along Beth's nerve ends and spread through her in ever-widening ripples of delight.

He kissed her eyes, licking away the tears her dream had brought on. "I never promised not to kiss you. Like this." He kissed her nose, her cheeks, the point of her chin. "Or like this." He kissed each corner of her trembling mouth. "Or even like this."

His lips caught hers and nibbled and pressed, and when Beth finally responded by opening her mouth with a capitulating little cry, he took the kiss deeper with his tongue and devoured her with a hunger and need that left them both breathless and shaken.

"I never promised not to do that," Nick whispered hoarsely when at last he lifted his head. "And please don't ask me to, Elizabeth."

He drew back a bit more so he could look into her eyes. Between the moon outside and the night-light shining through the open bathroom door, there was plenty of light for her to see what he was feeling, even without the words. But Nick had apparently decided that it was time for him to speak.

"Please don't ask me not to hold you when it's plain you need to be held. When I know that you need me. Elizabeth—"

As he spoke, Beth had quieted in his arms, closing her eyes against a rush of emotion as he smoothed the side of her face with the palm of his hand.

"You are so beautiful to me," he whispered, his voice rough with the force of his emotion, an emotion that was making his hand and body tremble where it touched her own. Never would Beth have known, never would Beth have believed it possible that a man of such rugged and masculine strength could have such a boundless capacity for gentleness. More, that such a man could have the courage to show it and not seem less of a man.

Of the multitude of differences between Dominick McCullough and J. C. Christofferson, *that* was the most fundamental of all.

And it was the one thing against which Beth had no defense.

Cradled against Nick's reassuring strength, wrapped in his tender concern and lulled by the velvet-rough whisper of his voice, Beth felt something give inside of her. Something that had been unyielding and tight around her heart, protecting it, yes, but also keeping it trapped in the cold and harsh confines of anger, bitterness and fear.

"I know how much you've been hurt," Nick murmured, all the while smoothing her cheek, his thumb gently erasing the last traces of moisture. His eyes were fixed on hers with burning intensity. "All I ask is that you let me keep you from being hurt ever again. All I ask is to keep you safe. All I ask, all I want, Elizabeth, is *you.* Not just for now, not just for a year, but forever."

"Oh, Nick." Moved beyond words, Beth reached up to touch his cheek as he was touching hers. Gently, so gently. "I—"

"Hush." His smile was crooked, bittersweet. "I'm not asking you to give me anything in return, sweetheart. I'm not trying to pressure you. I just want you to know that I love you."

Chapter Ten

"*I love you.*"

With her hands full of lasagna noodles, Beth closed her eyes and heard again the husky rasp of Nick's voice as he whispered those words to her. And she savored again the feelings his words had called forth, the incredible joy that had made her gasp and fiercely clutch him to her.

For at that moment, hearing those sweet, sweet words from Nick for the second time, the sound and promise of them had gone straight to her heart.

She hadn't said the words back to him; her feelings were too new yet for that. But she had shown him. With her hands, her lips, with all of her body and soul she had shown Dominick how much he had come to mean to her.

And at the moment of no return, she had given herself to him completely and without reservation. She had reveled in Nick's ardor and had fueled it with passion and delight, touching him as he touched her, clinging to him, moving with him and, finally, crying out with him as, together, they surpassed ecstasy's summit and plummeted into sated oblivion.

The door hinges of the screened porch in back of the house screeched, violently startling Beth out of her pleasurable reverie. Her cheeks hot, her pulse rate off the chart, she thought she must have missed Nick and Jason's return walk across the yard in her dreamy state. Pressing a hand to her heart and drawing a deep, calming breath, she turned toward the door leading from porch to kitchen with a welcoming smile.

It momentarily faltered when not Nick, but his sister, Karen, entered the room. None of Nick's family, not even Sophie, had been seen or heard from in the five days since the wedding. It was a shock for Beth to have Karen, the most reserved—not to say hostile—of Nick's siblings, arrive unannounced and uninvited in her kitchen.

And immediately proceed to act as if she owned the place.

With a cool and casual "Hi," she set down a package wrapped in Christmas paper, shed her bulky down jacket and hung it on one of the pegs behind the door. "Nick around?"

"Ah..." Thoroughly disconcerted by the woman's blasé, almost rude, manner, it took Beth a moment to recover her poise. "Actually, I saw him go into the horse barn a little while ago. Would you, ah, would you like a cup of coffee while you're waiting?"

"No, that's all right. I'll have some tea. Excuse me." Reaching past the nonplussed Beth, she opened a cupboard door and matter-of-factly took out the jar with the tea bags and carried it over to the stove. Then she filled the kettle with water at the sink.

"If that's supper you're making," she said with a glance at the lasagna, "you're courting trouble. Nick's strictly a meat 'n' potatoes man."

"Oh?" Beth's hackles were beginning to rise in the face of Karen's obviously deliberate attempt to make her feel like an unwelcome intruder. "He raved about the risotto I made yesterday."

"Really." Pouring hot water over the tea bag in her mug, Karen sounded skeptical and bored. "I'm surprised Jean allows you in her kitchen."

"It's my kitchen now."

Karen ignored that. She replaced the lid on the jar of tea bags and set it back in the cupboard. "Where *is* Jean, anyway?"

"She and Cy went to their daughter's for Christmas."

"Already?" Karen helped herself to some cookies from the jar on the refrigerator, then sat down. "What'd you do, have a fight with her?"

Beth's anger went from simmer to boil. Her hands shook with it as she smoothed some foil over the lasagna dish and began to clean up the counter. The woman was being deliberately confrontational. But she took a deep breath and reminded herself that this was Nick's sister. And that in light of their rather rushed wedding, a bit of distrust and hostility were understandable. Nothing would be gained by snapping back.

She forced a light laugh. "Heavens no. Jean and I get along like a house on fire." She rinsed some utensils and put them in the dishwasher. "Once she realized that Nick was in good hands, we didn't have any trouble at all convincing her to take the vacation early."

"Phasing her out, are you?"

"No!"

"This ranch is Jean's life," Karen said angrily. "She's been with us forever...."

"And she'll continue to be!" Beth exclaimed with an agitated toss of the hand. "I don't—"

She broke off, realizing her imminent loss of self-control, and silently counted to three.

"Look, Karen," she said more quietly. "I have no intentions of changing the status quo around here. Not where Jean's concerned, nor in anything else concerning the ranch. But I *am* Nick's wife now...."

"And how did you manage that so fast, I'd like to know," Karen injected cynically.

"I didn't *manage* it at all," Beth said with quiet dignity. "It was Nick's idea...."

"And one you, no doubt, jumped on."

"As a matter of fact, I didn't jump on it at all."

"But he was so crazy in love with you, he wouldn't take no for an answer, I suppose."

"You got that right, little sister," said a gravelly male voice from the kitchen doorway, making both women start and turn their eyes that way in shock. "Not that it's any of your business."

Nick, his face wreathed in thunderclouds, tossed his hat on the counter and came to stand next to Beth. Putting an arm around her shoulders, he drew her against his side, all the while fixing his sister with a hard stare.

"You want to be welcome here, you'll treat my wife with respect. Is that clear?"

"But Nick—!" Karen protested, jumping to her feet, red-faced.

"No." Nick's tone was all uncompromising harshness. The rigidity of Beth's muscles, as well as the stricken expression on her face told him how much this confrontation was hurting and humiliating her. He felt an urge to take his sister and shake the stuffing out of her. "How dare you come here and interrogate her? Who the hell—?"

"Nick," Beth interrupted quietly, "please don't say any more."

Nick snapped his eyes from his sister and looked at Beth. His expression softened. "I won't have you hurt. Not by anyone."

"I'm all right," Beth assured him, summoning a smile to prove it. "Please let me handle this myself."

Nick scowled in hesitation, then gave in with a curt nod. "What're you going to tell her?"

"The truth."

"The truth, huh?" He searched her expression. "You sure?"

Beth nodded. "Unless you'd still rather I didn't."

"No, go ahead." He met her shaky smile with one of his crooked ones. "I guess maybe it wasn't too smart keeping the facts from the family in the first place. Caused you unnecessary grief."

Releasing Beth, he walked over to where Karen stood watching them with obviously mixed feelings. He touched her cheek with his knuckles in a gruff caress. "Beth's a good woman, baby sister. Just as you are."

He left the kitchen, but turned at the door to say, "By the way, Jason's still out in the barn, 'helping' Cole and Jared. I'll be in the den."

"Please sit down again," Beth said after the kitchen door closed behind Nick. "Please," she added, when Karen, visibly fighting tears now, made a blind move toward the other door, the one through which she'd come. "I'd really like to talk to you. To explain..."

"You don't have to." Karen stopped, but didn't return to her seat. "Only tell me this, are you in love with my brother?"

Once again the other woman's bluntness rendered Beth momentarily speechless. Yes, she was in love with Dominick McCullough, but she hadn't yet told him so. Would it be right, then, to tell his sister? She decided that in the name of family peace, yes, it was.

"I am now."

"Meaning you weren't before?"

"That's right."

"The marriage wasn't a love match on your part?"

"No, it wasn't. Not on—" *Not on either part,* she wanted to add, but Karen didn't give her the chance.

"I knew it!" she cried triumphantly. "I just knew it."

"You know nothing!" Beth exclaimed. "Will you just listen for a moment? It wasn't about money, our getting married, and, true, it wasn't about love. It was..."

Faltering in the face of her sister-in-law's disdainful stare, and getting a bit fed up with the woman's high-and-mighty attitude, Beth decided to change tactics.

"Tell me," she said quietly, "is it me you object to, or would any woman Nick chose to marry have come under attack?"

"Excuse me? Attack?"

"Yes," Beth said, folding her arms and squarely facing the other woman. "Attack. Oh, nothing overt, just a pronounced chill from the moment we met. You made it obvious you didn't like to see Nick with a woman. And when he announced our wedding plans, you immediately became downright hostile, and I'd like to know why, since you don't know anything about me."

"I know you have a son."

"So? Nick loves children. He's always wanted a son."

"Of his own," Karen said vehemently. "Not some little gold digger's brat."

"That's enough!" Beth said sharply. "You don't know anything about us, because if you did, you'd know that Jason is a very wonderful little boy. He is not a brat and I am no gold digger and no one, not even Dominick McCullough's overindulged baby sister is going to say we are. Now—"

Stalking over to the table, she yanked out a chair. "If you really care about your brother and his happiness, I suggest you sit down and listen. If not..."

Beth's gesture toward the door was eloquent. Shaking inside with anger and dismay, she turned her back and went to pour herself a cup of coffee. Her hand trembled so much, however, most of the liquid ended up sloshing over. The carafe clattered to the counter. Beth pressed a hand to her forehead and strove for calm.

"Here," Karen said suddenly from right beside her. "Let me get that for you."

Beth dropped her hand but remained wary. She wasn't sure if she could trust this sudden about-face. For several long moments the two women stared into each other's eyes. Karen's were just like Nick's, clear and blue like a prairie sky on a sunny day. Just then they held Nick's somberness, too. But, more importantly to Beth, they held remorse.

"I'm sorry," Karen said, hesitantly handing Beth the cup of coffee she'd poured. "And you're right, I *had* made up my mind not to like you, to think the worst of you. But I could see the way you looked at Nick when he was in the kitchen here, and the way he looked at you..."

She paused, and then, rather drolly, burst out, "Darn it, I wanted him to marry Helen Kennedy."

"Helen Kennedy?" By now Beth knew most of the people in and around Starville, but Helen Kennedy was a stranger.

"She lives in Spokane now," Karen explained, looking sheepish now rather than angry. "She's my best friend. Divorced. Nick used to see her, though he always did say she wasn't for him. At least, not in a permanent way. But I kept hoping anyway, thinking with time..."

She made a face. "I've been such a pill. Sophie said so all along and Nan's read me the riot act, too."

Laughing a little, she swiped at her eyes with the back of her hand. "I'm not really as bitchy as I've been to you, generally speaking. There's even some people who think I'm pretty okay, most of the time."

"I never doubted it." Beth felt almost giddy with relief and was full of forgiveness and ready affection. "And I don't really blame you for mistrusting my motives in marrying your brother. After all I'm new in town. Nobody knows anything about me...."

"I'd really like to, though," Karen said seriously. "If you still want to tell me."

"It's kind of a long story," Beth warned her, taking her coffee to the table and taking a seat. "And it's not very pleasant."

They were both teary-eyed again by the time Beth had finished.

"Mom!" The door burst open and Jason, struggling mightily to hang on to a huge cat with other ideas, exploded into the room. "Look what I—" He broke off, visibly alarmed by his mother's tears. The cat took advantage of his momentary inattention to make her getaway.

"What's wrong, Mom? Why're you crying? Did—" He visibly swallowed. "Did Uncle Nick...?"

"Oh, God, no!" Heartsick at Jason's immediate conclusion that all men inflicted pain, Beth rushed to him and took him in her arms. "Nick would never, *never* hurt anyone, sweetie. Most men wouldn't—only some who are sick and need help."

"Like Dad."

"Yes." Beth hugged him fiercely as Karen watched in silent commiseration. "Like Dad."

"Are they making him better in that place he's in now?" Jason asked, his voice muffled against her neck.

Beth closed her eyes on a heartfelt prayer. "I hope so, sweetie. I really, really do."

After winning Karen over to her side, the rest of the family was suddenly eager to welcome Beth into their midst, as well. The next day, led by Sophie and Maynard, they all trooped over to the Triple Creek bearing figurative olive branches and very real, belated wedding gifts. Champagne corks flew, spirits were high. Christmas was only three days away; peace and goodwill were everyone's credo. Karen had brought a sprig of mistletoe and, unbeknownst to Beth and Nick, had hung it in the archway between the living and dining rooms. Everyone cheered when Maynard caught Beth beneath it and soundly kissed her.

They cheered even louder when Beth caught hold of Nick as he made his way into the living room. Laughing, holding his head between her two hands, she raised onto tiptoe, planted a noisy smacker on his lips and would have released him and stepped back if Nick had allowed it.

He didn't. His smile turning wicked, he kept her in place with one hand while he set down his glass and then, unencumbered, swept her into a passionate embrace. Beth's startled shriek ended half-formed and was swallowed by Nick as he covered the rounded "O" of her mouth with his own.

Her senses awhirl, her knees fast turning to jelly from the heat and intensity of Dominick's kiss, Beth threw her arms around his neck and clung like a vine to his strength. Forgetting their audience, she returned the kiss with enthusiastic fervor and was incapable of rational thought, when at last Nick released her lips and lifted his head a fraction.

"I love you," she murmured, staring into his eyes, feeling dazed and dreamy. She saw his eyes widen, darken, begin to smolder and felt a responding heat swamp her entire body.

"I love you," she said again, but half of the whispered declaration was cut off by the ferocious swoop of Nick's mouth.

It was hard, hot and short, this kiss. It was possessive, a brand, a claiming and giving. It was a promise, a vow, a portent of even better things to come. Because both Beth and Nick knew that with this kiss their marriage had finally begun.

Chapter Eleven

Christmas with all the family over at Sophie and Maynard's was, for Beth and Jason, like something right out of a storybook. On Christmas Eve everyone helped decorate the huge blue spruce with strings of freshly popped corn, gaily colored crystal balls and garlands of gold. Carols were sung and stockings were hung. And later, when one by one the youngsters ran out of steam and were bundled off to bed and into sleeping bags, the adults relaxed in front of the fire, feeling peaceful and blessed.

Beth and Dominick, thanks to their newlywed status, were given the only guest room, and on the aging mattress of the standard double bed, made slow and sweet love till well into the night.

A fairy time followed in the week between holidays. More snow fell. Thanks to particularly treacherous road conditions, few people ventured out of their homes and none did so just to visit.

The McCulloughs—Dominick, Beth and Jason—were content to have it so. They were intent on becoming a family, on tightening the bonds of love that, increasingly, bound them so that no one, from outside or in, would ever be able to sever them.

If thoughts of J. C. Christofferson intruded at times into their quiet idyll, they were quickly banished. Beth and Jason were safe with Nick. Trouble would never find them here on his ranch.

The weather broke on the second day of the new year, a Tuesday. Though it was bitter cold, the sun shone brightly from an azure sky, turning the thick, rippling blanket of white into a sparkling sea of diamonds.

Snowplows clearing the roads had created man-high walls of snow on each side, obscuring the usual miles-long, three-hundred-and-sixty-degree view of the countryside as two days later, on Thursday, Beth, driving the ranch pickup, followed the tracks of Nick's four-wheel-drive Jeep toward town.

Nick had—not very happily—set out for Spokane earlier that morning. A cattleman's meeting would keep him away from home overnight. He had wanted Beth to go with him, but with Jean still away and the ranch cupboards growing bare after their days of snowbound isolation, Beth had opted for a day of housecleaning and grocery shopping, instead.

With only a few more days of vacation, Jason had, predictably, chosen to stay at the ranch with the men who were more than willing to have the eager little guy tag after them, "helping."

Wheeling her shopping cart briskly up and down the cramped aisles of Mueller's Mercantile, her first official excursion into town as Mrs. Dominick McCullough, Beth decided being a rancher's wife felt pretty good. If some of the people seemed wary and a little slow in returning her cheery hello's, why, that was to be expected and not to be taken personally. They would come around, given time, just as Nick's family had.

Her shopping done and the bags piled on the passenger seat of the truck, Beth stopped in at Nedda's for a cup of tea and a visit.

There were only a few customers in the diner, despite the fact that it was nearly lunchtime, so Nedda and the girls, and even Charley Rider, were able to take a few minutes off for a jaw.

After the weather, as well as everybody's Christmas and New Year's, had been rehashed, Nedda elbowed Charley in the ribs with a broad wink.

"Say, Beth," she drawled. "Who's the good-lookin' fella who come around asking after you yesterday afternoon? An old beau, hmm?

"Beth, honey, what's the matter?" she exclaimed when Beth leapt to her feet with a gasp.

For a moment, Beth couldn't speak. She just gripped Nedda's arm and stared at her, light-headed and dizzy as the blood rushed out of her head.

"You're as white as a sheet," Nedda said, snapping in an aside to Stacy, "Quick, get the girl some water. Sit down, honey," she urged Beth.

But Beth, fighting the debilitating, panic-induced weakness that possessed her with everything she had, shook off Nedda's hand.

"What—" She swallowed, the terrible premonition making it almost impossible to get the words out. "What did you tell him?"

Nedda blinked. "Who?"

"That man." Beth gripped Nedda's arm again, shaking it. "What did he want? What did you tell him? Nedda . . . !"

"You're hurting my arm, hon." Beth instantly released her and Nedda rubbed her arm. She shrugged, her expression mildly peeved and very puzzled. "Why, I told him you're Mrs. Dominick McCullough, what else?"

"Oh my God." Beth pressed a hand to her throat. "And then what?"

"Why, then I gave him directions to the Triple Creek."

Beth didn't stick around to ask what this "old friend" of hers had looked like; she knew. She couldn't think beyond the fact that Jason was at the ranch with neither Nick nor herself to protect him. She jumped into the pickup, swearing aloud as she dropped the key her trembling hand was trying to insert into the ignition. She picked it up off the floor and took several deep breaths to calm herself and steady her hand enough to get the truck started. Gears grinding, she slammed into Drive and spun away from the curb.

Driving at breakneck speed toward the ranch, the pickup skidded and shimmied more than once. Beth didn't care; in fact, she barely registered any of her surroundings. All of her concentration was focused on Jason. Teeth clenched, hands welded to the steering wheel and accelerator pressed to the floor, she willed the boy to be safe. She willed him to be in the barn with some of the hands, helping with whatever chore they might be doing, willed him to stay out of sight.

Turning off the road into the long ranch drive, she almost crashed into one of the walls of snow. Only some wrestling with the steering wheel and a huge dose of luck enabled Beth to gain control of the sliding and fishtailing truck.

Shaken, but without letting up on the gas, Beth roared into the ranch yard. The truck bucked like an unbroken bronco when she jumped on the brake, slammed the gear into Park and, without killing the engine, slid out of the truck at a dead run.

"Jason!" She burst into the house, calling his name as she raced through the rooms. He wasn't there.

Far from being reassured— Had J.C. been here already? Had he taken their son?—she ran out into the yard and flew to the barn.

"Jason!" She tore open the door and let it slam shut behind her, startling man and beast alike into turning their heads to stare at her.

She spotted old Cole Ferguson in the entrance to the tack room. He was craning his neck out the door, wearing a puzzled frown over the commotion Beth was causing.

"Miz McCullough?" he queried, stopping to spit as he squinted at her. "Sumpin' wrong?"

"Where's Jason?" Beth demanded, chest heaving as she struggled for breath. "Where... Oh, Jason," she exclaimed as her son squeezed past the burly old ranch hand. Dropping to her knees, she hugged him to her. "I've been so worried."

"Why?" Jason and Cole asked in unison before Jason added, "What's the matter, Mom?"

Beyond speech for a moment, Beth bit her lip and, closing her eyes, brusquely shook her head as she held her boy tight.

"Sumpin' I can do for ya, missus?" Cole asked solicitously.

"No." Opening her eyes to look into his concerned face, Beth once more shook her head. "I'm okay. Now that I know Jason is."

She relaxed her grip on the boy and sat back on her heels. She brushed a hank of hair off his forehead and gave him a kiss.

Predictably, he squirmed out of her embrace with a mortified glance at Cole and a disgusted, "Mo-om!" At the ripe old age of eight, Jason had a hearty dislike of what he called "mushy stuff" being displayed in public. "Hey, I got work to do," he said and ducked back into the tack room.

As Beth got to her feet, she and Cole exchanged wry glances. "I should've known better," Beth said dryly.

The old cowboy spat again, then grinned. "Fine young fella you got there."

"I know. And I don't want to lose him." Beth dusted off her knees. "Anybody come by while I was gone?"

"Matter o' fact," Cole said and Beth's heart leapt into her throat. "Some city feller stopped by...."

"Oh my God. What did he want?"

"Didn't talk to him m'self."

"Then who did?"

"Jared met up with him at the barn door. Feller was asking was the boss around."

"And?" Beth impatiently prompted when Cole stopped for another spit. "What did Jared tell him?"

Cole looked surprised by the question. He shrugged. "Boss's gone, what else?"

"And that was it? The man left?"

"No. Heard him ask was you home or had you gone with the boss and Jared told him, no." Cole shrugged. "The feller said thankee and skedaddled."

"He didn't ask about Jason?"

"Nope."

Beth was certain that the man had been J.C. It was just the kind of thing he would do, drive onto the ranch bold as brass and ask for the boss. What better way to get the lay of the land? If Nick had been home, he would undoubtedly have come up with some innocuous pretext for the visit, then take his leave to wait for another, better chance to get at her and Jason.

Oh, yes, the man talking to Jared had been J.C., all right. And though Cole was telling her he had gone, Beth was far from reassured. On the contrary, she was desperately afraid because J.C. now knew that Nick was away and that she hadn't gone with him. In other words, that she would be back.

With a horrible feeling of dread, Beth knew without a doubt that J.C. would be, too.

She and Jason had to get away from here. No sooner had the thought formed, than she was calling her son and hustling him out of the barn. He was protesting loudly, but Beth ignored him, her mind busy with plans.

Just as soon as she was in the house, she would call the sheriff and alert him to the situation. J.C. was under a permanent restraining order and would be arrested again if he dared to come near her. Next, she would throw a few overnight things for herself and Jason into a bag and drive over to Sophie and Maynard's. There they would stay until Nick came back.

"Jason, stop complaining," she exclaimed with some exasperation when her son continued to loudly protest about being dragged away from his "work" in the barn. She ushered him ahead of herself into the house, saying, "Your father has been asking about us in Starville. In fact, I'm pretty sure he's been here at the ranch, too. Do you want him to find us?"

"No!" Jason, pale now and frightened, shot his mother an appalled glance.

"Well, then, hurry. Get your pj's and toothbrush while I call the sheriff's office. Hurry!"

She pushed him toward his room and rushed to the phone in the den. Grabbing up the handset, she clumsily stabbed 9-1-1 with a finger that shook and, taking a deep breath, put the receiver to her ear.

There was no ring.

With a groan of impatient frustration, Beth disconnected the call and, willing her finger not to shake this time, punched the three digits again with slow deliberation. And waited. No ring.

"I cut the wire."

Oh my God. He's here.

Beth stood like a statue, immobilized by shock.

"You won't be needing this, babe, will you?" the well-remembered voice of her nightmares drawled into her ear as a large masculine hand reached across her shoulder and roughly yanked the phone out of her grip. With something like a snarl, he tossed it aside.

It hit the hearth with a clatter that snapped Beth out of her momentary paralysis.

"Get out," she seethed, spinning to face her nemesis. "Get away from us. Get out of this house!"

"Or else, what?" he said with a sneer, catching her wrist in a vicelike grip as she raised a hand to shove him aside and run.

"Or else my husband—"

"*I'm* your husband," he snarled. "And I'm not going anywhere without you, my sweet *wife.*"

The appellation was accompanied by a twist of Beth's arm that was so vicious, tears sprang to her eyes. She clenched her teeth to keep from crying out, knowing from experience that any weakness she showed would only make him hurt her more.

With a wrenching jerk, he forced her arm behind her back.

"Come on, *wife,* let's go find our son, shall we? Let's be a family again." Pushing with his body against her back, he propelled her forward.

"Let go of me." Beth twisted in his grip, which only worsened the pain. Blindly, she kicked out behind her and knew a measure of satisfaction when her booted foot connected with his shin and elicited a grunt of pain. Her satisfaction was short-lived. Agony speared through her as he retaliated by giving her arm another vicious twist. Biting her lip, she stumbled forward.

"Which way, wife?" J.C. growled before raising his voice to shout, "Jason! Get out here! Now!"

"No!" Beth shrieked, trying harder to twist out of his grip. "Jason, run! Get to the barn. Get hel—"

"Shut up!" Her words were cut off by the hard hand he slammed over her mouth. She felt as if her jaw would crack from the pressure of his hand.

"Son!" he shouted. "You leave this house and I'll have to hurt your mother. Now is that what you want?"

"You let go of her!" Jason exploded into the room and launched himself at his father. Sobbing, he pummeled the man with his fists and kicked with his feet.

"Still Mommy's little soldier, eh?" J.C. snatched his hand off Beth's mouth and sent the boy sprawling.

Blood gushing from his nose, Jason lay stunned for a moment during which Beth twisted and fought against J.C.'s hold like a madwoman. With a violent shove, he sent her sprawling on top of her son.

Making a grab for Jason, she hugged him to her and stared up at J.C. "You're an animal," she spat, her voice vibrating with the loathing she felt for him. "Worse than an animal, you're a monster."

He stared down at her with coldly murderous intent. "Get up."

Beth didn't move, only glared at him with an icy contempt that seemed to enrage him anew.

"I said, get up!" he shouted, and bent down to haul her to her feet. He had her by the arm and was yanking her upright when a crash could be heard from the front of the house.

Seconds later there were shouts. Booted feet were running toward them.

Letting go of Beth, J.C. spun just as Dominick McCullough burst into the den.

Nick took in the scene in one glance—his wife on her knees and Jason cowering on the floor, the maddened man now facing him with fists at the ready. Without stopping for thought, he let fly with a mean upper cut that connected smartly with the other man's chin, making his head snap back and his feet stagger backward. Pressing his advantage, Nick followed the punch with a left into the man's gut and a knee to the groin that had him doubling over. He finished him off with a well-placed chop to the back of the neck.

J. C. Christofferson crumpled to the floor, hugging his midriff.

Nick barely spared him a glance. He dropped down in front of Beth and Jason and, with an inarticulate exclamation gathered them into his arms. For several long moments he only held on.

"Dear God," he whispered into Beth's hair, when at last he trusted his voice not to quaver and break when he spoke. "I thought I'd lost you. Lost you both."

He drew back and, as Beth did the same and their eyes met, he caught her lips in a fierce and possessive kiss. Her wince, and the taste of blood, brought the kiss to an instant and abrupt halt.

"You're hurt." Angling his head, Nick checked out Beth's face. Fury boiled when he saw the damage Christofferson had done. Both of Beth's lips were split and bleeding. An already purpling bruise discolored her jaw and her right cheek bore three bleeding, crescent-shaped cuts where the man's fingernails had dug in. "I'd like to kill him."

"No, Nick. Shh." Beth laid a soothing hand along the flexing muscle in Nick's rugged cheek and, catching his gaze, flicked hers meaningfully toward Jason, still huddled against them and shaking with reaction and fright.

Nick instantly got her drift. Worthless scum or not, Christofferson was the boy's father. It wouldn't do for Nick, who hoped to earn the right to be a *real* father to Jason one day, to go around spouting off about killing the man who'd sired him.

He gently caught the boy's chin, taking in pallor and wobbly lip and had to tamp down another spurt of murderous rage in response to it. With his thumb, he gently wiped a tear from the little boy's cheek and looked steadily into the large, fear-rounded eyes.

"I don't really mean that, you know," he said quietly. "Violence only begets more violence and is never the answer to anything." He tossed a glance at the man still doubled over on the floor. "See what I mean?"

Jason nodded, though a little dubiously. "I'm not sorry I hit him, though," he said after a bit of very visible inner debating. "Even if it did begets me a sore head. He was hurting my mom again and I'd promised her I wouldn't let him do that anymore."

Nick had to stifle a smile and swallow a lump, all at the same time. He was touched to the heart by the little guy's brave determination to protect his mother. Giving in to impulse, he leaned down and pressed a kiss on Jason's forehead. "You did just fine, son."

Beside him, Beth gasped. "Nick!"

And then a deadly voice grated, "Get the hell away from my wife and kid."

Lightning quick, Nick was on his feet. "Don't be an idiot, Christofferson. The game's up."

He spun to face the other man—only to find a gun pointed at his midsection.

"You're right, McCullough," J.C. drawled. "The game *is* up. Liz," Christofferson ordered Beth, keeping the gun and his eyes leveled at Nick. "Get the kid and walk out the front door."

"What're you going to do?" Beth demanded. She didn't move, except to tighten her grip on her son. "J.C., please. Don't—"

"Shut up and do what I said or so help me, I'll shoot him where he stands," Christofferson growled. "Now move!"

"Do as he says, Beth," Nick told her, never taking his eyes off the gun.

Beth was beside herself. How could she leave Nick with a madman's gun pointed at him? Yet what could she do? J.C. had sworn he'd shoot if she disobeyed....

Made awkward by fear and her aching bones, but with her mind racing, Beth scrambled to her feet. She bent as though to help Jason up off the floor, but, at the last second, spun around and threw herself against Christofferson's arm.

There followed a crash. A shot. Somebody screamed—it might have been her. But Beth really didn't have time to wonder, or to care. Something sharp and unyielding painfully connected with her skull, and that was that.

* * *

Voices drifted in and out of Beth's dreams. Restlessly, she stirred. She really wished people would be a little more considerate. After all, she was trying to get some sleep here. She was so tired. Her entire body ached with it. Every limb was weighted with a fatigue so heavy, it felt like lead flowed through her veins instead of blood.

Blood. There'd been so much of it on Jason's face. His poor little nose. J.C. might have broken it....

J.C.

"No!" she screamed, struggling upward through the fog and against the heaviness of her limbs. "Run, Jason! Ruuunnn...!"

"Hush, darlin'." Gentle hands were holding her flailing arms. A warm, husky baritone made soothing noises and spoke comforting words. "It's all right now, li'l Betsy. You're all right. Nick's here with you. You're fine."

Nick's here, Beth thought, quieting. *I'm fine.*

She slept.

The next time she awoke, there was no lead in her bones and there were no voices. There was only silence. Well, not quite silence, Beth decided, after lying still and listening for a moment. From over on the right, some deep, even breathing could be heard.

Beth rolled her head toward the sound and winced as a sharp pain shot through her skull. She closed her eyes a moment until the pain lessened. When she opened them again, it took a moment to adjust to the murky gloom of dusk. Or was it dawn? As her eyes adjusted, she recognized the man who was breathing so deeply in exhausted sleep. A rush of gladness and love made her heart expand.

Nick.

He was sitting in the big easy chair of the ranch's master bedroom, scooted close to where she lay on the bed. Why? She frowned and that hurt, too, making her wonder. What had happened? Jason...?

Jason. *J.C.*

In a flash it all rushed back into memory. J.C. He had found them. They'd fought. Nick had come. The gun...! A shot. Had she been shot? Who...?

She moved restlessly, moaning.

"Elizabeth?" Beside her, Nick came awake with a start and bent over her. "Elizabeth, are you all right?"

"Nick." Blindly, her eyes still closed against the pain, Beth reached for him. Her hands raced over his torso, his shoulders, his face. Her eyes opened, delved into his that were so close, so concerned, so full of love. "Oh, Nick... You're all right. Jason?"

"He's fine, too. Sophie has him."

"Oh, good. We were so scared."

"You were magnificent, both of you."

"No," Beth argued. "It was you. However did you get here? Why did you come back?"

"'Bout halfway to Spokane I got this feeling," Nick said. "A premonition, like. I just knew I had to turn back...."

"I'm glad."

"Me, too."

For a moment they just drank each other in. Glad to be together. Thankful for their love.

And then Beth asked, "J.C?"

"Sheriff's got him. I'd called him from my car phone. He got here in time to wrap things up."

"What about the shot?"

"It went wide. A hole in the wall." Nick cupped her cheek. "Guess you'll have to redecorate, sweetheart."

Beth managed a weak smile; the knowledge that her loved ones were unhurt had lightened her spirits considerably. "Too bad he didn't shoot the living room."

Nick dropped a kiss on the tip of her nose. "If that's your backhanded way of sayin' you want to redecorate the living room, too, go for it. Hell—" he kissed her again "—do the whole damn house."

"What happened to my head?"

"You whacked it pretty good on the edge of the hearth."

"How's the hearth?"

Nick grinned. "In better shape than you are. Which reminds me. Doc said to ask you what your name was, just to be sure you're not in shock. What's your name, sweetheart?"

"Elizabeth."

"Elizabeth what?"

"Elizabeth McCullough." Beth looked into his eyes. They were filled with concern and brimming with love. And she considered herself the luckiest woman alive.

"I am your wife, Dominick McCullough," she said tenderly, drawing him down to her and offering her lips.

He looked down at them, still swollen, though the blood had been wiped away. "Isn't your mouth still sore?"

"A little. Why?"

"'Cause I badly need to kiss you, honey, but I don't want to hurt you."

Very softly, he put his lips on hers. Their tongue tips touched, and something inside Nick ripped wide open.

"God," he burst out in an agonized voice, pressing his face against Beth's throat. "Elizabeth. I don't know what I would've done if I'd lost you."

He lifted his head. His eyes were brilliant with unshed tears. "I love you, Elizabeth McCullough. I love you so much. Will you stay with me? Forever?"

Her throat tight with emotion, Beth nodded. "Forever," she said hoarsely and gave herself up to Nick's long, tender kiss.

* * * * *

MILLION DOLLAR SWEEPSTAKES (III)

No purchase necessary. To enter, follow the directions published. Method of entry may vary. For eligibility, entries must be received no later than March 31, 1996. No liability is assumed for printing errors, lost, late or misdirected entries. Odds of winning are determined by the number of eligible entries distributed and received. Prizewinners will be determined no later than June 30, 1996.

Sweepstakes open to residents of the U.S. (except Puerto Rico), Canada, Europe and Taiwan who are 18 years of age or older. All applicable laws and regulations apply. Sweepstakes offer void wherever prohibited by law. Values of all prizes are in U.S. currency. This sweepstakes is presented by Torstar Corp., its subsidiaries and affiliates, in conjunction with book, merchandise and/or product offerings. For a copy of the Official Rules send a self-addressed, stamped envelope (WA residents need not affix return postage) to: MILLION DOLLAR SWEEPSTAKES (III) Rules, P.O. Box 4573, Blair, NE 68009, USA.

EXTRA BONUS PRIZE DRAWING

No purchase necessary. The Extra Bonus Prize will be awarded in a random drawing to be conducted no later than 5/30/96 from among all entries received. To qualify, entries must be received by 3/31/96 and comply with published directions. Drawing open to residents of the U.S. (except Puerto Rico), Canada, Europe and Taiwan who are 18 years of age or older. All applicable laws and regulations apply; offer void wherever prohibited by law. Odds of winning are dependent upon number of eligibile entries received. Prize is valued in U.S. currency. The offer is presented by Torstar Corp., its subsidiaries and affiliates in conjunction with book, merchandise and/or product offering. For a copy of the Official Rules governing this sweepstakes, send a self-addressed, stamped envelope (WA residents need not affix return postage) to: Extra Bonus Prize Drawing Rules, P.O. Box 4590, Blair, NE 68009, USA.

SWP-S994